After Sunset

Clayton Hanson

To My Mother

ACKNOWLEDGMENTS

I would like to thank the following:
My family for their love and support.
My brother, Coby, for pushing me to write a book.
Rhonda Gardner, teacher extraordinaire and all-around awesome person, for being an inspiration in literature and in life.
Emily Ethridge for making the book better.
Foster and Julie Foster for everything.
And a special thanks to Hayley King for her dedication to making the book better and for repeatedly telling me, "I'm not sure what this means…"

INTRODUCTION

The events in this book happened. The conversations have been taken from notes and journal entries. The only event that may be a bit fuzzy is when I got my ass kicked by a woman.

CHAPTER 1

Washington, DC is the most heavily guarded metro area in the United States, and outside of Jerusalem and the Vatican, the world.

The Metro Police Department's First District reaches from the White House through Capitol Hill to RFK Stadium, south to where the Potomac and Anacostia rivers meet, and north to Florida Avenue.

The MPD has assigned more than 400 officers to the "Fighting First" and shares jurisdiction with the following: the Supreme Court Police, the Secret Service and the Uniformed Division of the Secret Service, the National Park Police, the U.S. Capitol Police, the Smithsonian Police, the Library of Congress Police, the U.S. Mint Police, the DEA, the FBI, the Federal Protective Service and the Metro Transit Police.

I learned this in my capacity as a Legislative Liaison for the Department of Homeland Security. When I would tell people outside of the DC Beltway that I worked for Homeland Security, they would start out interested and some would think that I was a badass by association until I told them I worked in the legislative division. Then their eyes would gloss over and I would change the subject.

That's all in the past now.

Now that I've changed, none of the gun-toting officers would be able stop me. I could literally rip someone's head off. I've done it.

CHAPTER 2

I used to wake up every weekday waiting for the weekend or waiting for Congress to go into recess or some combination of both. The other departments in the DHS looked down on mine. We had political pull but the other sections considered us children who were raised with silver spoons in our mouths because our bosses were political appointees and not bureaucrats. We were on the same floor as the buzz-cut militants in the Secret Service and the hyperactive spazzes of Federal Emergency Management Agency. The guys from the Secret Service were too cool to acknowledge anyone else's existence even though it was our efforts with congressional appropriators and the White House that kept them funded. The FEMA folks were so consumed with running mock catastrophic scenarios that they failed to realize that none of their make-believe incidents had ever or will ever happen. They say they couldn't have predicted a hurricane the size of Katrina, but they have ran hundreds of mock disasters (nukes, toxic terrorist attacks, etc.) involving baseball parks and other densely populated areas.

I used to wish we worked on the same floor as the Transportation Security Administration (called the crotch grabbers by my boss) because it's impossible not to feel superior to the guys who screen baggage at the airport and "randomly" screen good-looking women for pat-downs.

Every weekday I took the Metro rail downtown to our office. Taking the escalators down into the station brought a stench of stale air to my face from out of the tunnel. I felt like I was descending into an underground bio-chemical plant that the government couldn't put above ground because they didn't want to risk killing the surrounding civilian population. Other dangerous things underground for the safety of all mankind include nuclear contaminants, sewage and hell. All of them are better options than riding the Metro.

The trains are generally clean (by public transportation standards) but I couldn't stand being around a lot of people in a cramped space. In the summer the trains stink because the passengers huff and puff through unbearable heat and humidity before getting on the train. In the winter people cough and sneeze without covering their mouths in an effort to infect me with some deadly disease. Then again, maybe I have been hanging out with the hypochondriacs from FEMA too much.

After surviving the pitfalls of public transportation, I would buzz into my office building with my security card and then go through the metal detector. I started carrying a bag when I worked there because it was easier to dump my phone, watch, wallet and keys into it instead of having to drop everything into a plastic bowl and then dig it all out after. There was nothing more annoying than waiting at one of the machines because some jackass who has to go through the scanner every single day couldn't pull himself together and figure out why he kept setting the alarm off.

When I arrived at my floor I would wander though the maze of gray cubes until I got to mine. The good thing about my location was that if some how a gunman made it onto our floor there is no way that they could find me. It took me a week to be able to find my cube on my own. The only downside was that the felt cubicle walls weren't much protection.

On my last day, even though I didn't know it at the time, I couldn't bring myself to open my e-mail program because I knew there would be e-mails from my workhorse colleagues who labored through the weekend. On a typical Monday there would be at least seventy e-mails waiting for me, but compared to some of my colleagues and their two hundred e-mails, my load was light.

I gazed at the home screen for a minute, started to nod off, and then got up to get a cup of coffee.

I was glad that my coffee mug was dirty because it added a few extra minutes for me to clean it, which let me stay away from my computer for a little longer. Over the weekend the sugar had glued itself to the bottom of my cup and the time that it took me to scrub it out helped me relax. Then I filled the cup with low-grade government-issue coffee and wandered back to my cubicle. I had hoped to find someone to talk to on the way back to my desk to but it wasn't in the cards. At that point, I would have talked to anyone about their weekend.

Eventually I opened my e-mail program and was watching it fill up with e-mails from Saturday and Sunday when Megan came over.

"Hey dickhole. Thanks for showing up on Saturday."

Megan overcompensated for her cute femininity by having the foulest mouth of any person I had ever met. There were only two other females on the floor, and as the youngest by thirty years, she had learned to ward off the ill intentions of the men we worked with by insulting them with amusing anatomical sayings based on the penis. She was charming, but I wasn't mentally ready to deal with her first thing on a Monday morning.

"Oh yeah," I said. "I forgot."

One of our coworkers had a party and I told people that I was going to go but I didn't show up. My colleagues are nice enough people, but the last thing I want to talk about when I'm not at work is work.

"Mmmhmmm," she said. "You've been here for over a year now and I don't think you've ever remembered to attend a party."

"Probably," I said. "How about a drink or seven after work?"

"Maybe. I'll see you at the meetings."

"What meetings?"

"Do you ever look at the group calendar?"

"Yes, well, no."

"We have the Homeland Advisory Council from 9:30 to 11:30 and then the Data Privacy and Integrity meeting from 12:00 to 5:00."

"Ah fuck."

"We had meetings about the meetings last week."

"I know, I know, I forgot." Then I turned towards my computer. "All right, then I have work to do."

Then she walked away.

Our meetings were held in rooms named for famous politicians, but the space had little or nothing to do with the namesakes, unless Polk and Jefferson were involved with mass production furniture covered in bagels, fruit chunks and coffee.

Before the two meetings, we had meetings to discuss what we were going to discuss at each meeting. We also went over the agenda and action items. A person unfamiliar with government work would think that a gathering we spent so much time preparing for would have gone well, but they would be wrong.

A few of the department heads, responsible for making decisions, sent their minions who had no decision-making power whatsoever. When the minions were asked for their department's input they blushed and said that they would have to talk to their bosses. Another department, actually had its boss there, but he had to have questions repeated to him because he was on his phone checking his e-mail the whole time.

All in all, both meetings went rather well compared to the usual.

By the time I got off I was ready to have a drink, and fortunately DC is made for happy hours. It has a fiscally poor population (entry-level jobs on the Hill pay crap) that dealing the monotony and frustration of politics, combined with the inefficiencies of government work. It's the perfect blend for a potential alcoholic. In addition, most of the staff is either just out of college or has only been out a few years so they still drink like college students with no responsibilities.

While we were in our meetings Congress passed our authorizing legislation, which meant that we were funded for another year. A department-wide email went out announcing that there would be a party and we went to our typical happy hour spot.

It was also cause for my section to celebrate because we had a fight with a few members of Congress and their staff about "Shall" versus "May" clauses in a bill. If a bill says "May" then a department may or may not do the mandate, but if the bill says "Shall" the department has to do whatever the bill says.

Our marching orders from the Secretary were to get as many "Mays" in legislation that pertained to us as possible so that he could control his agenda. I understand how boring it sounds to people who live outside of the Beltway but this is how the sausage is made, so to speak. Going out that night, the only item on the agenda was getting drunk. People in DC will use any reason they can find to break out of their tight, structured shells.

After a few celebratory shots I decided to start some shit with my co-workers. It isn't that I didn't like them all the time, just not when I was drunk.

"Hey Billy," I said to one of the ridiculously thin terrorist assessment guys. I was a few drinks deep and determined not to be ignored.

"Willie, Billy, Billiam!" I bellowed, getting louder with each name. He finally looked up at me.

"Hurricane Katrina and Ike caused more damage and cost to the American people than all of the 9/11 attacks combined," I said, "so wouldn't it be more cost-effective to build better storm protection in the Gulf Coast than it would be for the other heightened security measures in the whole country?"

"Here we go again," said Megan, who was sitting next to me. "Why do you have to antagonize the nerds? It's like we're in high school."

"I bet we will have another natural disaster before we have another terrorist attack?" I ignored Megan. "What do you want to bet, 2 to 1? I'll bet $100 against your $50?"

"Yeah," said Billy/Willie, "because we'll prevent it."

"Okay Jack Bauer. You've prevented sooooo many attacks. I'm just saying that America would benefit more per dollar if you could figure out how to prevent hurricanes. We both know you didn't stop shit. Me and Chris saw you fall while walking up the stairs two days ago so don't act like you're out there cuffing and stuffing bad guys."

"Why do you have to antagonize those guys?" said Megan pulling me away while trying to hold back her laughter.

"They think they are so badass and all they do is sit and analyze reams of info." I had a slight slur in my voice. The seams of my sobriety were unraveling.

"You and the damn hurricanes," said Megan.

"But…"

"I don't want to hear about it," she said cutting me off. "I'm calling it a night. Are you done?"

"I'm done with this place. Buncha chumps."

"Help me find a cab."

"You help me find a cab."

"Oh my knight in shining armor. What would I do without you?"

"Probably bang one of those anal…yst dorks."

"Ha. You wish. Then I would never hear the end of it from you."

"Damn right."

As we were leaving I tried to go out a door that was locked and I slammed into it like a bird into a window

"Come on genius." Then she pulled me out of the unlocked door.

We went outside and there was a cab already waiting.

"You can catch a ride with me if you want."

"I'm not done yet. I'm going to The Pour House. You in?

"It's 10:30 on a Monday so no."

"All right. Later tater."

For a moment I almost hugged her but instead we stood there looking at each other awkwardly from a few feet away. Then she got into the cab and left. I stood outside in the rain. It was cold out, but not quite cold enough to snow. A breeze from the west cut right through my pants and suit jacket. I started to walk up the Hill when a cabbie honked at me to see if I needed a ride. I jumped in.

When I got to The Pour House there was a steady stream of people leaving. I went upstairs to meet my friends.

The upstairs part of The Pour House is a typical DC bar. It's slender in width and long in length, with sticky wood floors and a hint of old beer smell from years of drunken staffers spilling everywhere. Coming up the stairs, the bar is to the right and to the left is a pool table and a random assortment of couches and mismatched tables and chairs.

My buddies had a table. I made my rounds by shaking hands and saying, "Doctor" and in return the guys said doctor back to me in reference to the movie *Spies Like Us*. Quoting movies is one of the few things that bind male friendships. The others are drinking and chasing women.

"How's everybody doing?" I said.

"Good," said Craig with a smile. Craig was the elder statesman who had been working on the Hill for the past fourteen years and had been married for the last ten. He was out for his one "boys night" a week as allowed by his wife. While he didn't ever chase women, he didn't mind looking.

Andrew came up with a bucket of Miller Lites and put them in the center of the table.

Brandon said, "Three o'clock." Brandon was a good-looking fellow who found joy in burning bridges with every woman he ever slept with.

We used a clock system to identify where to look so that we wouldn't have to point or describe the person we were looking at. It took a little calculating because you would have to look at the person who is calling out the time and then figure out how to read their clock. If someone is sitting directly across the table from you, their three o'clock is your nine o'clock.

"Your three is lame," Andrew said, "Check my midnight."

"I slept with your midnight," Brandon said.

"No way," Craig said.

"Hey Summer, why don't you come over here and give Daddy a hug?" Brandon yelled to a girl with black hair standing at the bar.

She gave him the finger and then turned her back on the table.

"Yeah." I said, "He definitely slept with her."

"Jesus." Andrew said, "What did you do to her?"

"A little bit of this, and a little bit of that." Brandon said while making hand motions that I don't need to describe.

Craig ordered a round of SoCo and lime shots for the table. Whenever there is a group of guys, it's always the married one who wants to drink the most. They want to prove that they can still drink and they have the biggest need to blow off steam.

Then this gorgeous, petite blonde came in by herself and took a seat at the bar. She was so gorgeous that I wasn't able to say the time on the clock for her location to alert the other guys. She had an air of confidence that moved people away from her. She was short and blonde with choppy hair that reminded me of Tinkerbelle. Not the horse-toothed Julia Roberts version of Tinkerbelle, a hot one.

Craig swiveled his chair a little so he could get a better look at her.

"Two two two," said Craig, calling out the time in rapid-fire fashion.

His frantic number calling alerted the others to look at the same moment she turned to look at us. We were morons.

"She just looked at me," I said, "I'm pretty sure she is into me." That was a lie. I was talking shit.

"Not a chance," Brandon said. "A lady like her will steal your soul. By the time she's done with you, you'll wish you had never met her."

"So the same way you make girls feel about you?" Andrew said to Brandon.

"It's true though, she wants me." I said, "She looked right at me and then her ring finger twitched, just a little bit. She's already thinking about our wedding."

Even though I knew she couldn't hear us due to the loud music and the people talking all around her, it seemed like she smiled to herself when I said that.

"Go talk to her then," Andrew said. "Or are you going to sit here all day and make daydream babies with her in your head."

"Okay, I'm going," I said.

"Then go," Craig said.

"Shut up," I said.

Around the fourth beer of the night we would start acting like thirteen year-old boys.

"$20 you can't get her number," Brandon said.

"You're on," I said.

I got up and walked over to the bar. My stomach felt light and I started to blush a little. I wanted to bail out because trying to pick up girls at the bar is the worst. I never knew what to say and I always think that I'm going to go down in flames in front of the whole bar. On the way over I wanted to check to make sure that my fly was up because I was getting self-conscious but grabbing my crotch on my way over to introduce myself didn't seem like a good idea.

I walked up to her and said, "Hi."

"Hi," she responded with a smile.

"Do you think I'm cute yet or should I buy you a shot?" I said.

"A shot?" She slowly looked me up and down. "Maybe two. No wait. Three."

"Yes!" I said, "I'm in."

I figured if I was going to go down, then I might as well go down in flames.

"It's a little early for that kind of talk, don't you think?" She said.

"No, um, no, I didn't mean in, in. Like this." Then I made the forefinger through the other hand giving the okay sign, how an eighth grader would indicate sex.

She started to laugh. "Please stop." Then she put her hand over both of my hands so that I would quit gesturing.

I remember thinking that her hands were cold but I didn't think anything of it at the time. Ladies always have cold hands.

"So can I get you that drink?"

"No no. I think I have had quite enough for tonight."

"Oh, okay. Oh yeah, my name is Stephen. It is pronounced Steven, but spelled Ste-fen, but with a P-H."

"I'm not sure if what you said makes sense but I'm going to let it slide. I'm Charlie. You pronounce it the same way you would think to spell it."

"Yeah, you know, from across the room, I thought to myself, Stephen, I bet that girl's name is Charles or maybe Chuck."

"When you talk to yourself you use your name? Is that to get your own attention?"

"I guess so."

I was confused and by the time I figured out what she meant the conversation had moved on. Remember, I had been drinking.

"Instead of drinking more, do you want to go for a walk? The music in here is giving me a headache."

"Yeah, sure."

"Do you need to go by your table to get the $20 or will your friend give it to you later?"

"Wow," I said, "you heard that? Awkward."

"Yep."

"No, I can get it from him later."

I waited for her to call me an asshole and walk off but she didn't. Instead, she got off of her barstool, grabbed my hand and headed towards the stairs to leave, dragging me behind her. I remember giving Brandon the finger before I left while Andrew smiled at me and Craig shook his head.

After I left the bar, all of the drinks and shots caught up to me and my memory goes fuzzy.

CHAPTER 3

The next night I woke up and it was dark out. My first thought was that it was the morning, but when I turned on the TV, the evening news was on. Somehow I had slept through the whole day even though I was an early riser. As a bureaucrat I was used to getting up at seven in the morning.

I shifted in my bed and my whole body felt like it was on fire. I had a migraine from hell. The thump from my heartbeat inside my skull was loud and overwhelming. It was difficult to separate out the cacophony of sounds and smells of basic existence but once I was able to do so, I could hear the sound of blood being pumped through my dog's heart. My first instinct was to leap across the room and attack her but I was stopped by my overwhelming need to puke.

I sprinted across the hall to the bathroom and vomited into the toilet until there was nothing left but dry heaves. I realized that due to the force of my vomiting I had shit and pissed myself as well. Dinner the night before consisted of a peanut butter and jelly sandwich and chips before I went out drinking so it couldn't have been food poisoning. I peeled off my clothes and jumped in the shower to wash off the filth.

While coming out of the shower and I watched the steam from the shower roll out into the rest of the bathroom. It wasn't a translucent mass of fog anymore. It was individual particles of floating water and I could see tiny little rainbows reflecting through them. I expected to be cold due to the winter chill in the house but I wasn't cold at all.

The phone rang.

"Hey man," I said. My phone had seven voicemails on it.

"Hey, hey, hey," said Brandon. "I called earlier to see if you wanted to hit up lunch with a bunch of us but you didn't answer."

"Yeah, I'm just waking up," I said.

"What? Seriously?" he said. "It is like 6 pm."

"I know. I'm dying over here. I think I was tired from this week at work or something. Are you as hungover as I am?"

"I'm good," he said. "We ate at Fatty's for lunch and it got me through rest of the work day."

"Nice. I'm starving."

"So what happened with that blonde?"

"I honestly don't remember. I woke up at home. Help me out here."

"I don't know. You didn't introduce us. She was pretty hot. I thought you took her home."

"She might have came home with me, I don't know," I said, "Were we drinking tequila or something? My memory's completely blank."

"Yeah, tequila made a showing. So did some Jameson's and a little Southern Comfort and lime."

"Jesus. I'm getting too old for this." I said. "Let me pull myself together and I'll call you later."

"All right, later."

I put my phone down on the desk and looked at it curiously. There were two voicemails from Megan, four from my work and one from Andrew. I didn't listen to them because the dog hadn't been out since the night before and she was whining at the door. I put on a hooded-sweatshirt, a coat and some jeans and took Diablo (my dog, not Satan) outside for a walk.

While adjusting my coat I saw a hair tie on the floor. I picked it up and set it on the kitchen counter. I didn't bother trying to think about the events that transpired the night before because of my headache.

I was putting the leash on the dog while I opened the door to my house. Diablo saw her chance and made a run for it. For the first time I was able to catch up to her and grab her collar before she got to the end of the yard. I was quickly distracted by the fact that the door to my house was open and I still needed to leash her up. I couldn't keep my thoughts straight. Sensory overload made me feel like I was going out of my mind, but I chalked it up to a super-charged hangover.

I didn't think about it at the time, but I wouldn't ever see the sun again.

We got to the park and I let Diablo off her leash. She liked for me to chase her but for the first time, I caught her. I got right behind her and pulled on her tail a bit, which made her run even faster. We were in full out sprint mode and I knew I could overtake her, but we were running out of park to run through. I didn't even get winded.

I slowed down because I noticed a lady on the far side of the park watching us. I looked behind us and there were fallen leaves floating in the air like in a cartoon. I put my hands on my knees and acted like I was sucking wind for a little bit. There was no reason to show the world that I was a freak on my first day.

Even though I wasn't sure how it happened, I now knew how Peter Parker felt the first time he realized that he was Spiderman.

As we walked away from the lady who saw us running, a young brunette had cut across the park and was heading towards us. Instead of feeling lust, I wanted to drink her blood. We passed within a few feet of each other and I smelled her perfume. I heard her strained breath from walking fast. I learned later that when people breathe like that it's because of asthma. My fangs came out for the first time. They didn't pop out like they would later; I felt them growing as she got closer. I didn't notice until they were crowding my mouth. Without thinking, I turned and started to reach for her. I wasn't thinking about the consequences. It was pure instinct. I was hungry. My hand was a few inches from her neck when I pulled it back. Her crimson scarf blew in the breeze and she reached up and patted her hair down. When she turned and looked at us, we were walking away, minding our own business. She had no idea that she passed within inches of becoming my first meal.

At that moment I realized was a vampire.

I didn't snatch up the young lady in the scarf but I was still hungry. After I took Diablo home, I went back into the night. I tried not to think about it at the time, but I was going out to find blood.

It wasn't the usual hunger pangs. I could feel it in my whole body, all the way down to my fingertips. My skin felt tight and dry. The old me thought my new craving for blood was disgusting but it was all I could think about. I was a junkie looking for a blood fix.

Walking east towards the Congressional Cemetery, I didn't have a specific destination in mind but I wanted to head away from the Capitol and all of the extra police and cameras. The cemetery is next to the DC jail and a couple of housing projects, so there were plenty of people to choose from and almost all of them avoided contact with the authorities. I didn't have a plan but I knew that whatever happened, I didn't want anyone watching.

I was walking on E Street between 13th and 14th when I saw a girl walking the same direction as me.

She had a long ponytail and was wearing a fluffy pink coat and jeans. She was in that ambiguous age where I couldn't tell if she was 12 or 16. I followed her across Kentucky Avenue. On some level I was aware of how creepy and strange I was acting, stalking this girl, but that didn't matter because my hunger was stronger than all of my other emotions combined.

Now I recognize the feeling as needing to feed but at the time I hadn't felt like a starving animal before. When I'm that hungry I'm on the verge spiraling out of control.

I closed the distance between us. My patience was wearing thin and my hunger had taken over. There was a gap between row houses where dump trucks could fit between the houses to unload the trash bins in the back. Most people in DC don't want to put their trash on the curb like some commoner. The general sentiment was out of sight, out of mind.

My timing was horrible. I wanted to take her into the alley smoothly but my hunger had taken away my ability to think clearly. As I was crossing the street I didn't see the curb and I stumbled at the unexpected drop off. I staggered a few steps as my forward momentum gained speed, and took over causing me to fall on my face.

The girl hadn't been aware of me until I said, "Oh shit." Then she looked at me. Instead of dusting myself off and trying to play it cool, I got up and made eye contact.

The look in her eyes told me that she knew I had bad intentions. She didn't know that I was going to drink her blood, but her natural flight instinct kicked in.

The stalking part of my hunt was over, I ran straight for her. She didn't stand a chance. I leaped over a parked car and landed a few feet behind her. She started to scream but I grabbed her throat and all that came out was an "awwkkkk" sound. She tried to fight me off but she was too weak.

I grabbed the hood of her jacket. With my other hand still around her neck I dragged her into the alley. I felt her panicky heartbeat radiating off of her whole body. I was so hungry that I didn't bother taking her deep into the shadows. Anyone who was walking or driving by would have seen me. I tilted her head to the side and sunk my fangs into her carotid artery. Her blood gushed into my mouth.

At that moment I thought about when my father taught me how to ride a bike. We were standing at the top of this huge, grassy hill when he put a motorcycle helmet on my head. I remember being scared until my dad looked at me and said, "Just hang on tight son and everything should work out fine." He must have saw fear in my eyes because he let out his laugh that was like a sonic boom from the bottom of his belly. Then he gave me a little shove without warning me. Somehow after barreling down the hill I was able to ride without training wheels. It was the biggest thrill of my life at the time and changed my life permanently.

The first taste of her warm blood was fantastic. It had a hint of cinnamon.

She went limp. I kept drinking until she was dead. When I was done I let her fall to the ground with a thump. All of a sudden it hit me what had happened and I felt sick. I retched once and threw up most of the into a storm drain.

I couldn't believe what I had done. I had killed an innocent person for my own needs. I knew that I would have felt differently about killing her if she was dying or if she had been a criminal, but this was out of hunger and nothing else.

In the future I would have to be a more discriminating and not so careless. I didn't want to end up in jail or dead or both.

Distraught, I wandered aimlessly. I had a hard time coming to terms with being a monster. Cheating on girlfriends (twice) or stealing things (more than twice) didn't even come close to the amount immorality that I had committed. I wasn't violent by nature. I hadn't even been in a fight before. I couldn't help but wonder what my friends and family would think.

Time flew by while I was lost in my thoughts. I looked at my watch and realized that I had no idea when the sun was supposed to come up. The sky was getting lighter so I knew that I didn't have time to make it home. I was down by the baseball stadium that was at least a couple miles away. I started jogging, looking around frantically. I felt the temperature start to rise. I crossed under I-395 and looked at the spaces under the overpass but there wasn't anywhere to hide. The last thing I wanted (other than cooking in the sun) was to be found and considered dead. I might wake up while some coroner was removing my guts to weigh them or whatever it is that they do. I found a full dumpster next to a school and jumped in.

My super sense of smell really worked against me but I didn't have another choice. I pulled a bunch of bags on top of me and wiggled my way to the bottom, so in case someone looked into the dumpster they wouldn't see me.

I woke up some time after the sun had set and had the distinct feeling that the dumpster was moving. My suspicions were confirmed when I saw streetlights passing overhead.

While I was able to recognize what was going on, I wasn't used to how vampires sleep. It's like a light switch was flipped and I was asleep. The same applied to waking up. At one moment I was asleep and then boom, I was awake. Vamps don't get drowsy. I think I had dreams but I couldn't recall them the next day like I could before I had turned. The only common thread in all of my dreams was that everything moved fast while my feet were stuck in concrete. People moved around me, taunting me in a language that I couldn't understand, but from their posture I knew that they intended to hurt me.

Then I had an epiphany; I realized that I was in the back of a nasty smelling dump truck. I looked down and my left hand was black and shriveled like a raisin due to exposure to the sun. Even though I had no proof, I knew that was the case. I had survived the day and needed to get out of this truck so I could figure out where I was.

I stood on top of the bags but they kept shifting with the bounces and turns of the truck so I couldn't see over the sidewall. Some time passed and finally the garbage truck came to a stop. I had no idea where I was, but I wasn't going to find out by hanging out in the back of a dump truck. I leapt out of the back and landed on the hood of a big, mint green Mercedes.

Once I was out of the dump truck I still didn't know where I was. The driver slammed on his brakes and started to get out. The lady he was with stared at me in shock. I couldn't blame her. Before he could get all the way out of the car I yelled, "Sorry," and ran the opposite direction. A street sign told me that I was on Shadyside Lane. I didn't know if I was in Maryland or Virginia, but it didn't matter because there isn't a difference in the Metro DC area. Besides, lost is lost.

The guy turned his car around and came after me, so I cut between some houses and came out the next block over, on a street called Lazy Lane. I jumped a few fences and ran a few blocks. I wasn't doing much about finding my way back home but at least I had lost the Mercedes with my two size 12 footprints on the hood.

I started walking up the street. The lower-class residential neighborhood was full of two-story row houses and only every other house decided to take care of their lawn. Fortunately the area is full of commuters, which meant that there were lots of signs to lead them to the nearest interstate.

Eventually I ran into Maryland Route 4 which turns into Pennsylvania Avenue. The same Pennsylvania Avenue that the President of the United States lives on. I finally knew where I was and had a road that I could follow into the city.

During the ruckus of getting chased, my formerly charred hand had healed a little. It was red and there was some blood flowing in it. It looked more like a craisin instead of a raisin and I considered it an improvement.

It took me over an hour to jog home. I didn't sweat but I was mentally exhausted. Getting chased stressed me out more than I had thought it would.

Afterwards, I set my phone alarm to play "Hear Comes the Sun" by the Beatles. I found a phone application that would have my alarm go off one hour before the sunrise so that I wouldn't have to climb into another dumpster.

CHAPTER 4

My first week as a vampire was a blur, only punctuated by a voicemail from my boss.

"Hey, we haven't heard from you in a week, so per our HR policy we are going to have to let you go. A few employees have seen you wandering about so I guess you aren't sick. You know I don't want to do this, but we have to. We can't have employees not showing up. We will mail you your last paycheck stub."

I had meant to give my boss a call but I didn't know what to say. I was basically dead during office hours so I wouldn't have been able to work something out. He was a nice guy but not really cut out to lead people. Like a lot of government management he was more concerned with keeping his job than managing people.

I didn't really like my job but then again, no one does. I would rather not go if given the option. I missed being a part of something. I had already started to feel isolated from my friends and family and now I wouldn't have coworkers to bond with over our bosses' incompetence.

Recently I had moved into an English basement owned by my best friend, Andrew and his wife of a year, Anne. I felt guilty living under him with my condition while he was trying to start a new life with his wife. It isn't like I could've moved out. I didn't have anywhere to go. I couldn't find a new place to live. I slept during the day and leasing offices aren't open at night.

I hadn't figured out a way to tell him that I was a creature of the night although on some level his wife already knew. Maybe not consciously but somewhere down deep where she didn't want to confront it, she knew that she should be afraid of me. Ever since my change people looked at me differently. At first I thought I was being paranoid because I had changed and was aware of it. I could hear a conversation from across the bar or smell whether someone decided to put on deodorant so every little change in body language was apparent. Somehow people knew that they should be afraid of me, they just couldn't pinpoint the reason why. Aside from my paleness, my physical appearance was no different than anyone else's.

Babies and animals knew to be afraid of me and didn't care why. I had to avoid babies when I was at the store because they would point at me and start crying. Their mothers would apologize and mumble something about "I don't know what has gotten into him (or her) today". I would smile and keep moving. Even my dog that I had since she was a puppy didn't have the same playfulness with me.

It was a pain in the ass not being able to go out in the sunlight. I couldn't hold down a regular job and if I worked the door or bartended at some club it wouldn't cover my student loans, rent and car insurance. Plus I don't know how to bartend and spending eight hours a night behind a bar would be a waste of my new powers. In an expensive city like Washington, DC, $15 an hour wasn't going to cut it.

I considered robbing a jewelry store, but they have cameras and I figured there might be people looking for someone with my description after I killed the girl. I didn't see any witnesses to my crime but the city had too many people for someone not to notice.

Also, I didn't know what to do with the merchandise. Perhaps I could stand on the street corner like some stereotypical goon with my coat open hawking watches. I didn't know anyone who had access to the black market. All of my friends were bureaucrats or lobbyists. I didn't even know what the black market looked like. I imagined it was a big warehouse filled up like a flea market with stolen goods, but that couldn't be right.

My bills were piling up. I needed to pay my rent so I decided to mug someone. I felt bad about the prospect but I didn't have another choice. I told myself that I would only do it this one time and then I would find a better source of income.

I couldn't rob anyone on Capitol Hill because the neighborhood was too small, so I went to Dupont Circle. Riding the Metro rail up there was out of the question because there were cameras all over the system. On the off chance that the cops decided to look for a mugger, I didn't want to be noticed.

On my walk northwest up Massachusetts Avenue I looked for people to rob, but I didn't have any chances because it's a major street with too much traffic. By the time I was in Dupont Circle my nerves were frazzled from sensory overload. It was hard to focus which so much going on. The headlights, taillights and all of the honking, honking, honking, made me feel like I was getting an aneurysm. I thought that if I heard one more person honk I would break his damn neck.

I walked west on P Street and after few blocks I found an ATM that I could see from an alley. I walked around the block psyching myself up, trying to convince myself that this was the only way that I could make rent. I saw an older couple walking in front of me on the other side of the street, crossing the threshold of the alley.

Running across the street, I passed close enough to the back of a moving car to hear the buttons on my coat click off of the rear bumper. In a flash, I grabbed the man by the back of his coat, wrapped my arm around his wife and forced them deep into the alley, tossing them on the far side of a dumpster. The only sound was the wife, saying "Wwwhhaaa". I think she was going to say "what" but the rest of the "tttt" got held up in the process.

I pinned the man against the wall by the back of his neck with my right hand and picked up his wife by the front of her coat with my left hand. She was so small that I didn't realize her feet weren't touching the ground until I looked down. She searched my eyes to try to see who I was but I had wrapped my scarf high up on my face and pulled my winter hat pulled down. The less of me they saw the better.

I had read that vampires are able to hypnotize people by looking into their eyes. I wasn't able to perform that trick but the look between the wife and I felt pretty close. She was completely under my control.

"When I put you down, you're going to hand me your wallet and your cell phone, is that clear?" I said.

She nodded yes.

"Please don't run, because then I'll have to break your neck," I said. I nodded at her husband still pinned up against the wall, letting her know that he would pay the price as well.

"Grab his wallet," I said.

"Let me go," he said gasping. He was trying to wiggle and create a little space for himself but I held him tight.

"Quiet," I said.

She stopped and looked at the back of his neck and then handed me his wallet. I grabbed his credit cards and let the rest of the wallet fall to the ground.

"What's your PIN?" I said to the husband.

He paused, like he had a choice in whether he was going to tell me or not. I pulled him back a few inches and slammed him against the wall hard enough to make his nose drip blood. He groaned pretty loudly and I worried that a passerby would hear us and call the cops.

"8, 9, 2, 4," he said.

The lady started to back away from me. She was getting close to being out of my reach so I grabbed her by the front of her coat.

"You're going to withdraw all the money that you can out of the ATM from his cards and any cards that you have as well. Don't make a sound. Blink twice if you understand," I said as quietly as possible so that we wouldn't attract attention.

Blink blink.

"I'm going to watch you the whole time, and if you look at anyone else or try to get help, I'm going to start breaking his bones, one by one," I said. "We clear?"

Blink blink.

"Go," I said nodding towards the ATM. I watched her walk over. She looked down at her shoes the whole time.

When she came back something had changed in her eyes. She wasn't scared any more. She was pissed and I saw courage building in her posture. She didn't cower away from me.

"The money," I said.

She held her hand out, but held the money far enough away from me so that I would have to let her husband off the wall. I let go of her husband and turned on her. I picked her up by her coat and held her against wall so that we were eye to eye. I put my other hand on her neck and I felt the blood pumping through her veins. The man had turned towards me after I let him go but he was frozen in place with fear. I was face to face with her. She had her eyes closed.

"Look at me," I growled through my clenched teeth. I was doing all I could do not to shout at her. "Look at me!"

She opened her eyes as little as she possibly could. Her husband shifted his feet.

"Please don't make this process harder than it needs to be," I said to her. I looked at her husband. "Don't try to be a hero."

Then I let her down. Her hand still had the money in it. As soon as I put my hand on hers to take the money, she recoiled.

"Now the ring," I said, looking at her wedding ring.

She put her right hand over her ring finger for protection.

"Please no," she said with tears in her eyes.

The sad wet look in her eyes that made me feel miserable and ashamed. I took the money and ran off into the night. I wondered if every mortal that I met for the rest of my life would be afraid of me.

Whenever I've seen vampires on TV they are rich, brooding, teenage hunks and glamorous ladies, but if there is a How To Get Rich Manual for vampires, I haven't seen it. As for my looks, it's usually my humor that wins women over.

I thought that being a vampire would be more fun than it turned out to be. On TV there were vampire bars and other weird and interesting creatures (like werewolves) that vamps feuded with but that wasn't going on in DC.

I still had to pick up my dog's poop. There was something a little discombobulating about how she looked me in the eyes while she was using the bathroom, like she needed her privacy. Meanwhile she was going on the corner of Massachusetts and Constitution while traffic is bumper to bumper.

Vampires have to feed every week or so, but instead of finding humans to survive off of, I was draining stray cats and dogs. I didn't want to repeat the horror of the first time I fed on a human but I also couldn't stand the smell of the strays and their fur. Most of them tasted like sour milk from being sick. One of the dogs was so sick that I couldn't drink his blood. I broke his neck to put him out of his misery. He didn't even try to run from me like all of the others. When I walked up to him he rolled over on his back, resigned to his fate.

I woke up one evening and turned on the television out of habit. I was feeling a bit lonely and wanted to watch something comforting and normal. The news was on and even though I didn't watch it before I was turned, I was curious to hear about what had happened in the world while I slept. There was a story about a fire in Adams Morgan that destroyed an apartment building, and then the girl that I had fed off of appeared to the left of the talking head. I had tunnel vision and thought I was going to pass out. I didn't hear what the reporter said, but then they cut to a police officer at a press conference.

There was something about the way the cop looked into the camera and said that they had no suspects that assured me that he was lying. I felt him looking at me through the TV. His look made me feel like I was going to get caught. He mentioned the girl's name, Leanne Washington, which reverberated in my head a few times before I was able to push it out. The headlines would read "Monster From the Hill" (hopefully not Hill Monster because that would make me sound like a troll) or "DC Dracula Drains Daughter". The authorities would make me do a perp walk all chained up with a mask over my face like Hannibal Lecter. There was no way that I would get a fair trial. Outside, the church bells rang, signaling eight o'clock. The bell tolls for thee, I thought to myself.

After the broadcast I was nervous about going out and snatching another person off the street, so I went to a hospice that was on the south side of Pennsylvania Avenue.

The building was part of an old Section 8 housing unit (Section 8 is a federal program that provides with rental assistance to low-income families) that covered half of a city block. The other units around it had been knocked down to create parking for the surrounding residential area. The three-story building had been made without any aesthetical consideration: bleak grey with maroon trim that was fading into rust. The complex was an eyesore and one of the last reminders of the old neighborhood in a rapidly gentrifying area.

The back of the hospice building had a high wall with some trees facing I-395. One of the windows on the second floor was cracked open. I jumped up to the window and held on to the thick concrete sill. I could hear the heavy breathing of the sleeping occupant and the faint suck and wheeze of a ventilator. I pulled myself up and slowly opened the window. An elderly man's head was sticking out from the covers. He was long and gangly like a spider. I pulled myself into the room, stood in the corner, and watched him for a minute. Even if he opened his eyes, he may not have been able to see me. His heart-rate monitor was the only source of light in the room and the faint green display didn't create much light. I was wearing all black and had pulled my hood up over my head. I listened to his faint heartbeat corresponding with the monitor and wondered if he had enough blood pressure to feed me. Nurses down the hallway were discussing which patients they thought were going to die first, which was rather morbid even to me. Someone said it was going to be Margie, but my bet was on the guy in the room with me.

I crept into the hallway and walked down a few doors to look around. Most of the bedroom doors were open and most of the interior windows had their shades drawn putting the patients on display from the hallway. Each room had the same faded light green paint and the doors were outlined in dingy white paint. The only person with flowers was an older lady whose lone medical appendage was an IV.

The hospice was creepy and I was anxious to leave. I didn't fear getting caught by anyone because my senses were on high alert, but I was anxious because I was there to kill my first person since Leanne. I quieted my insecurities and focused on the sounds around me. If someone changed his or her breathing pattern within 50 feet of me, I would've heard it.

I went back into the man's room. I found his carotid artery and sunk my teeth in. There was a momentary rush of adrenaline accompanying the blood slowly pumping into my mouth. His heart monitor slowed to a stop and then the flat line alarm went off. I stood there for a moment looking at the husk of what used to be a barely living human and watched as the two puncture wounds slowly healed themselves. I went to the window and pulled it most of the way shut after me. As I descended to the ground I heard the soft jogging of sneakers combined with the huffing and puffing of the out-of-shape nurses responding to the alarm. I leapt from the brick wall and faded into the night. The thrill and the strength that I gained from the blood was tainted by the death of someone I didn't even know. The only positive, besides being fed, was that it didn't taste like a stray animal.

Afterwards, I went home. The snow had started to fall in little flakes just big enough to announce its presence. I was a few blocks away when I could hear the sounds of people having sex. At first I thought it was amusing until I recognized the lovemaking sounds of my ex-girlfriend Christy. She was much too rich for my blood and I wouldn't have ever been able to give her the life that she had expected. When I thought about her it made the part of my life where I was a regular human seem like an eternity ago.

I was on my nightly stroll when I heard a voice. I wasn't sure of where it was coming from at first but it was loud enough to weave itself into all of the other sounds of the night.

"Goliath stood and shouted to the ranks of Israel, 'Why do you come out and line up for battle? Am I not a Philistine, and are you not the servants of Saul? Choose a man and have him come down to me,'" some holier than thou guy said.

Curious, I ran towards the voice. It was coming from a big, grey stone church. The church looked out of place. It was surrounded by row houses and cars like it had fallen out of the sky and landed there.

I leapt to the roof and landed with a thump. Then I hid behind the steeple so that if anyone came out to look at the roof to see what the noise was, the tops of the trees and the pitch of the roof would hide me. I sat down and listened to the sermon.

"After forty days David convinced his father to let him fight Goliath. From 1 Samuel 17:45, David said 'You come against me with sword and spear and javelin, but I come against you in the name of the Lord Almighty.'" The preacher continued, getting to the gist of his sermon, "David knew that with the Lord on his side he didn't need to fear anyone or anything. That was the true strength of this faith."

When I was growing up I did a little time in church, and the pastors failed to mention that after David killed Goliath he cut off his head and carried it around like he had won the Vince Lombardi Trophy while the Israelites plundered the Philistines' camp.

I started to get mad thinking about all the bullshit and half-truths that Christianity had told me, and how the clergy omitted the gory details. The fact that Christians don't follow the Bible even though they said that they believed in every word pissed me off. By their standards I was going to hell. While I was thinking about hell and how it was my destiny, I looked up and eight feet above my head was a stone cross, anchored into the steeple.

I jumped on top of the steeple and pushed on the horizontal part of the cross. The old stone budged a little.

These were the same people who would've burned me at the stake in the past.

I pushed a little harder.

These people would've burned down my house with me in it while I slept if they knew I existed.

I pushed and then pulled back towards me and the cross loosened a little more.

These are the same people who judged me even before I became a monster in their eyes, conveniently forgetting the all-important, "judge not lest ye be judged" part of their religion.

With a final push the cross broke free of its mooring.

The thought that I was going to hell and there was nothing I could do about it enraged me. My condition wasn't my fault.

I looked over the side of the roof and saw a black Escalade parked in front of the church, the perfect target. I threw the cross and it crushed the roof down to the seats. The glass exploded outward and for a moment the destruction was beautiful. The tiny broken shards of glass reflected the light in infinite shifting ways. The congregants came out to see what had happened, but by the time they were outside I was three blocks away, strolling down the street at mortal speed.

I woke up at sunset and turned on the news. I should have learned my lesson last time but I didn't. Before I could make it to the kitchen to feed Diablo and give her some water the news announcer said, "There is a person of interest in last month's murder of Leanne Washington. Police are looking for a white male that was seen leaving the area around the time of the murder. The police had this to say 'We are asking if anyone in the community who has any other information to please come forward and help us solve this heinous crime.'" The show cut back to the talking head who said, "A heinous crime indeed."

Heinous. Yeah, that pretty much summed it up. There wasn't anything that I could say in my defense like, "I didn't mean to slash her neck with my fangs and suck her dead." I'm sure that wouldn't play very well in the court of public opinion. I had thought that I had forgiven myself for killing her but I hadn't. I still felt guilty even though it was something that I didn't have any control over. The most disturbing part was that even if I did have control over myself, I would have killed her anyway.

CHAPTER 5

Before I was turned, I had a gun pulled on me in DC after a friend's party. A girl, Tristan, who I worked with at a bar who had graduated from Georgetown Law. To celebrate she had a party at her place. I didn't want to go but she was nice to me and graduating law school is a big deal so I sucked it up and went. When I had stayed a polite amount of time I decided to walk to the Metro. Her visiting mother and sisters were going the same way as I was so I decided to walk them back to their hotel. It wasn't sheer chivalry that propelled me. One of Tristan's sisters was a really pretty redhead. I didn't think that I had a chance with her or anything but I didn't see any harm in spending a little more time with her.

We decided to walk down 19th street NW, from T Street. The street was darker than it should have been because one of the streetlights had burned out. The rest of the sidewalk was in the dark because thick trees had grown underneath the lights. I might have thought that we should've taken another street but perhaps that is revisionist history.

For a long time, the mere thought of what happened next made me sweat.

We approached a boarded-up house that had a set of stairs at the end of the yard that was hidden by hedges. When I was a few steps away from the stairs, a guy jumped out from the steps with a gun.

"Holy shit, you scared me," I said starting to laugh it off. Then I saw his gun. He held his gun on me while the woman he was with went to all the ladies and grabbed their purses. I thought that I was going to see a flash of light from the muzzle blast and then I would be off to the big unknown.

The ladies gave up their purses pretty quickly but their mother hid behind me, using me as a human shield. She had a hold of my shirt in the back, and was playing tug of war with the male mugger who had a gun in my face. Without putting any thought to it, I reached behind me, grabbed the mother by the back of her shirt, and tilted her head up so that she could look into my glaring eyes. I said, "Give him the purse, Mom." She did. The woman mugger ran off while the guy backed away slowly and held eye contact with me to make sure that I wasn't going to do anything. I didn't. Then they were gone.

We filed a police report, but nothing substantial ever came of it. A detective called and asked me a few questions but he didn't follow up. I haven't ever forgotten the face of the man who robbed me. I saw him in my dreams for months afterward.

After I was robbed my feet didn't seem fast enough. Every time I was out past dark, my body clenched when I saw another male on the street. I'm ashamed to admit that I would cross to the other side of the street when I saw black guys coming my way. In my head I knew that, no matter what color, every single person that had passed me on the street, before and after, didn't rob me. But that didn't matter because I had looked down the barrel of a gun, waiting for a blast to end my life.

A few weeks after becoming immortal, I walked the streets at night because I didn't have much money and all of my friends had to work in the morning. Passing time sitting at home made me feel sorry for myself. Outside, I listened to the familiar sounds of people snoring, televisions blabbing and drunk people talking over each other when I heard someone say, "Give me your purse, bitch!"

I sprinted towards the corner of an apartment building and saw a woman with her back to me playing tug of war with a man who was cocking his fist to punch her. He threw the punch and I caught his fist mid-swing. Then I slammed him up against a parked car. The girl was still holding her purse, watching us.

"Run," I said. "Now."

She snapped her out of her shock and ran away, heels clicking into the night.

The guy started to get up. He was dazed but looking for a fight so I punched him in the ribs. He dropped to his knees, gasping for air. I grabbed him by the back of his neck and forced him to look me in my eyes. Then I backhanded him. Blood flew from his nose splattering the sidewalk. When I let him go he flopped to the ground, writhing around on his back trying to get a full breath. I stood over him, straddling him with my feet on both sides of his jacket so that he couldn't move.

"If I ever catch you or any of your friends out here fucking with people, I'm going to beat the shit of them," I said. "I'll be watching you."

When I reached down, he flinched, and I went through his pockets. I found a wallet and a set of keys. I wanted him to know what getting robbed felt like. I took them and got off of his jacket. He rolled into the fetal position. I stood over him trying to look into his eyes for a few moments but he was shielding himself from another attack. He stayed on the ground until I was around the corner.

As I walked away, I realized that I was being two-faced for punishing a robber after mugging a couple not too long before. But saving that woman made me feel good about myself, and it had been a long time since I had felt that way, so I tried not to dwell on it.

After getting a few voicemails from my mom, I called her back before she decided to fly down and chew me out personally. Growing up as the youngest, with a father that passed away, I had to learn to deal with my remaining parent giving me the attention of someone playing the role of both parents.

"Hi Mom," I said.

"Well, well, well. I guess you're alive," she said. I could tell that she had a smile on her face. I thought to myself, I'm not technically alive but that is beside the point.

"Yes, I am," I said. "Are you staying out of mischief?"

"I'm trying to but you know how that goes."

I asked her that question as a running joke between the two of us. She had been a stay at home mother for all of my life. My father died in an accident on an oilrig, and in exchange for never talking about the accident to the press, or anyone else for that matter, the oil company gave her enough money to live the rest of her life without having to work. It wasn't a huge sum but enough. We didn't talk about it much, but one night after some wine she told me that she would give all the money away and go back to work in exchange for one hug from my father. I was drunk enough at the time to tell her that for that amount of money she should hold out for a shag. She chuckled a little bit, rolled her eyes then got up to get another glass of wine.

"How are things down there?" She said.

"Oh you know, crack, murder, and extortion. And that's just the Members of Congress," I said.

"Ha." She loved corny jokes. "When are you moving home?" She asked me this every time we talked. She was joking when she asked, but she also wanted me to move home.

"The day that you tell me you have the dough for me to retire."

"That will be the day."

"Exactly."

"Okay Smartypants," she said. "I'm going to let you go."

"Is everything okay?" Our conversations usually lasted at least fifteen minutes.

"I'm feeling a bit under the weather so I'm going to rest for a bit, okay? I'll talk to you later."

"Okay. Later Tater."

Then she hung up.

After I stopped the mugging I decided that I would be a superhero. I would get a uniform and figure out how to make money from it, but those were just minor details when I was fantasizing. A few nights later I wandered over to Foggy Bottom because I was tired of being on the Hill. Somewhere off of 22nd Street I heard a guy pushing around a woman.

I made a note of the row house and watched it for a few days. There was a side garage surrounded by a wooden fence. I climbed to the roof of the garage and from the roof I could see into what must have been a little girl's room that had pink and white curtains with Power Puff girls on them.

A man came out to put trash in one of the trashcans when I jumped down from the roof and landed right behind him. I had nothing to fear. I created fear. I put my mouth next to his ear.

"So you like to push women tough guy?" I asked in a whisper.

"Who the fuck are you?" he said, turning around and dropping the trash bag he was carrying.

"Don't worry about who I am, Mr. Bad Ass," I said.

I pushed him into the row of trashcans he had lined up along the wooden fence along his driveway. He landed on top of them. One of the cans tipped over and a white trash bag poked its head out of the formerly covered can.

"Why don't you pick on someone your own size?" I said. "Come on pretty boy with your big phallic Lexus. You can push around women, so let's see how tough you are."

He got up and began to brush himself off. He wanted to fight but he wasn't used to fighting something that could beat him up. He was master of his household and he exercised his will over everyone who lived there, but now I was on his property and he knew he wasn't in control.

I closed the distance between us and kneed him in the nuts. Then I pushed him back on top of the knocked-over trashcans.

"What's going on out here?" said his wife who had appeared in the side door.

"No more," I said to the man.

I didn't look in her direction. I just ran away. As I was leaped over the fence I noticed a pair of brown eyes watching me from the window with the Power Puff Girl curtains.

I came back a few nights later and sat on the same part of the roof. I felt pretty good about myself. I would settle some domestic violence and make him learn to keep his hands to himself. While I was sitting there I heard rustling in the girl's room. The curtain opened a bit and there was elementary school-aged brunette with pretty brown eyes that were almost too big for her head. They were the same set of eyes that I had seen before the last time. She stared at me for a minute, then began to open the window very slowly. She winced when it squeaked and looked back at her door to make sure no one was coming. I could hear her parents were downstairs talking.

She leaned to put her mouth close to the window crack. "You have to go away."

"What?" I whispered.

"You are only making things worse," she said. "Now Ron is mad all of the time. Go away please. Okay?"

I hadn't ever dreamed that a voice so small could sound so forceful. I nodded and left. Short of killing the guy, I didn't have any other options. He would be able to hurt them during the day when I wasn't there.

My stint as a superhero was over. No one ever told Superman that he was making things worse.

CHAPTER 6

"Hey, douche, what are you drinking?" asked a pink-haired, chubby girl wearing a red and black latex-looking shirt that caused her to spill out of the top. I'm sure she thought she was being sassy and charming, if not to me then to the other patrons, but instead she came off as desperate and cliché.

I tried to think about what she had asked me but the atmosphere transfixed me. It felt more like I was on a movie set. People were acting the way that people expected them to act, not the way they wanted to act. It was reflective of DC as a whole.

After going to bars for weeks looking in pursuit of Charlie (I didn't know if it was her real name or not), I ducked into a little dive bar called Subterranean Jungle. There were mohawks and the assorted piercings of people who don't want to fit in with mainstream society but still wanted to fit in somewhere. A counter-culture culture. Neat.

"Whiskey, rocks," I said.

I leaned in close and took an audible sniff though it wasn't necessary.

"I can smell your period," I said. "Quite the heavy flow day my dear, maybe you should have that checked. And you should consider going easy on the tequila."

She leaned back from the bar and for a moment her tough façade was shattered. Her pupils dilated and she held her hands in front of her chest. Then she reached under the bar and poured my drink. She slid the glass across the bar without making eye contact. I dropped a $20 and left to find a corner where I could see everyone.

Even in my all black attire (the better to bleed you with my dear), the other customers looked at me like I didn't belong. They were right, I didn't belong there, but not for the reasons that they thought. For a self-conscious moment I wondered if I wasn't goth enough to be there until I remembered that I'm so goth that I can't go out in the sun or I would die so those posers could suck it.

As I negotiated my way to a different section of the bar, a short blond ran into me. I couldn't see her face but I could feel that she was like me. My spine tingled and my fangs came out. She moved through the crowd, weaving through people, using her small size to fit quickly through openings that were too small for me. I couldn't keep up without smashing into people.

I saw the door open and she was gone. I pushed through the crowd and went outside. There were a few smokers hanging around outside of with the sad, decrepit, industrial buildings that surrounded the area but the lady was no where to be found.

I figured that I might as well leave. I had no other reason to be at the bar. A few blocks later I heard someone in heels running across the roof of a building on the same side of the street as me. I ran into the alley between two of the buildings and jumped up the right side of the one wall, which propelled me up the wall on the left. From the left-side wall I was able to jump to the roof of the nine-story building. When I got to the top, she was standing there waiting for me.

She was the same petite blond from the bar, wearing jeans and dark red leather jacket. Despite her diminutive size she looked like she was made of nails. She couldn't have been more than 5'1" and a hundred pounds fully clothed and soaking wet, even though her heels gave her an extra artificial inch or two. She walked over to me and looked me up and down.

"Interesting trick to get up here," she said. "Did you have to practice that?"

"Not really," I said. "I couldn't think of another way."

I tried to sound cool but her confidence unnerved the hell out of me. I had gotten used to being the only monster in the night but now I was face to face with another one. For the second time since becoming a vampire, I wasn't in complete control. The first time was when I was feeding and I didn't have control of my body because I was trying to survive. This time I was scared, the same way that mortals must have felt about me.

"In time you will be able to jump up here. The longer you live, the stronger you'll get."

In what appeared even to me to be a flash, she pinned me to one of the nearby doors that led to the roof. We hit the steel door so hard that it buckled a little under the force. She held me by my jaw and pushed my head back, exposing my throat. Her fangs came out and she was licking her lips. Then she took a few steps back. She had shown me how easy it would be for her to kill me.

"Everyone that I have created goes to that ridiculous bar at some point. It took you much longer than I expected. I'm a little disappointed."

"I looked at quite a few other bars before this one," I said, a little annoyed at her implication that I was dumber than the rest of the people she turned. "How the hell was I supposed to know where to find you? You didn't leave anything behind so I've been going out every night looking for you."

"Oh come on now. We both know that you weren't always looking for me," she said. "You mugged some tourists, hypocritically beat the shit out of a mugger, and then you stepped in when that guy was beating his wife. That's pretty noble for someone who has to kill other humans to stay alive."

"I try. And I don't always kill humans." It unnerved me to find out that she had been watching me and I didn't notice.

"By the way, I killed the wife beater for you. I drained that piece of shit half dry and pushed him off of his roof. I checked their mail and he had life insurance policy so his wife and step-daughter will be fine."

"How?"

"How did I kill him? Easily. I waited until his ladies were out and then I cracked the window with my fist. When he came upstairs to see what was wrong, he opened the window and leaned out to see what had happened. Then I pulled him out of his house by his hair, emptied him then tossed him off the roof. It turned out that he had hair plugs. A few of them fell out when he hit the ground." Then she scrunched her nose in an adorable way that obscured the fact that she was talking about killing someone.

There was a lull in the conversation as we sized each other up. I didn't know if I was supposed to ask her why she made me like this or all the other questions that had plagued me since I had woken up as a monster.

"This is where you ask me why I made you this way."

I looked at her, trying to get a read on what she was thinking but it was no use.

"I did it for fun. I get lonely. When we met, you seemed like a great guy and you have lived up to it so far. To mortals, some of the things that you have done may seem ghastly, but in our world you almost qualify for sainthood."

I felt my anger rising.

"You didn't even ask me," I said. "How can you completely change someone's life without even talking to them or anything? You don't even know me. You fucked me over because you were lonely. Fuck you."

She flew at me and pinned me against the wall with my wrists. I struggled and couldn't even get them to flex. The most demeaning part was that her expression didn't show any effort at all. She slowly dragged her fangs down the front of my chest, tearing my shirt into two ribbons and drawing thin lines of blood. She looked up at me and licked the blood off of her teeth.

"Don't start getting sassy with me Sweetie. I can end you right now if I want. I doubt I would even work up a sweat. Well, we don't sweat, but I'm sure you understand the expression. I gave you the gift of immortal life and I expect you to be a little more appreciative."

"Did you ever think that maybe I don't want to live forever?" I said. "Now what am I supposed to do?"

"Survive for now. A lot of the men that I turn end up killing themselves or really screw themselves up trying. They can't handle it. They act like they are so brilliant and in control at the bar and the next week they are begging me to kill them. It's so sad." She had the same tone of someone asking to pass the salt. Then she put the back of her hand to her forehead and imitated a man's voice. "Oh the enormity of it all. What will I do if I can't go to the job I hate any more and spend ten hours a day with people who come and go out of my life?"

She started to walk slowly away from me. I was momentarily transfixed. She walked with the aggression and confidence of a mini-supermodel, almost stomping with each step. Then she jumped off of the roof and into the night.

My days had shifted. I was waking up around 6:30 or 7:00 depending on the sunset. Two in the morning was lunchtime.

I had worked up a bit of an appetite after playing with Diablo in the park. When I first turned I didn't know how she was going to react to me or how she was going to adjust to my new schedule, but as long as I took her out regularly and let her run around she was fine. She didn't want to be petted and she didn't need as much attention as she did before, but that was okay by me. She got to go outside and play more than she did when I had a regular job even though we played in the dark.

Once again I snuck into the hospice. There were a few people awake down the hall near the nurse's station at the end of the hallway. The noise from the front was filtered room by room. Everyone beyond the first few rooms were long asleep. I wish I could say it was a human smorgasbord, but it was more like going to Arby's late at night. It wasn't appetizing but it would keep me alive until I was able to get something better in my stomach.

There was an old black lady connected to a bunch of cords that caused her to look like a robot. I didn't want to drain her because I was worried about getting shocked by one of her devices.

An elderly white lady two doors down from the end of the hall was my next meal. Besides getting the blood I needed to live there was no thrill involved. I was ashamed to admit it then but I can admit it now: it was boring because there was no hunt. I might as well have drank a blood donor bag.

My money situation was becoming dire. My savings had been minimal before I was turned, and now they had run out. After watching the TV series *The Wire*, I decided that I was going to rob some drug dealers. They weren't hard to find in DC.

I waited until a Saturday night and took a stroll into a neighborhood in the Northeast. Before I had been turned I didn't dare go into that neighborhood. I saw a sign that said, "WARNING- Persons Coming Into This Area To Buy Drugs Are Subject to Arrest & Seizure of Their Vehicle" so I knew I was in the right place.

The drug dealer's setup was pretty easy. One guy took the money, one guy was the in-between who signaled how much drugs to give, and the last guy in the chain handed out the drugs.

My big black hooded sweatshirt was over my head so people couldn't see my face. I was a little concerned about limiting my sight but with my super hearing I figured that I would be fine. The shirt was my good luck charm. I had fed with it on and never had a problem.

I walked a few blocks, deep into the neighborhood, and only saw people sitting on their porches. A few guys may have been holding but no one made any offers.

There was a homeless man pushing a shopping cart into an alley. I thought about following him in there to drain him, but I had fed the day before so it wasn't necessary. I took a few steps down the alley and then jumped onto one of the rooftops of the houses that lined the streets. From up there I could see most of the street in front of me while being able to hide using the pitch of the roof. I would be able to see more of the street if I was to walk on the top of the roof, but then people looking up would be able to see me as well. I went from rooftop to rooftop, not having to jump because all of the houses were connected.

At the end of the block was an older-looking boy sitting on some concrete stairs that led out of the row house on the corner of a four-way stop. When certain cars would come to stop, he would run out to the car and put his hand into the passenger side window. Then he would point for the car to take a right turn, signal down the block and the car would then drive off. The whole transaction was done almost wordlessly. I couldn't hear much due to the distance between us and because the cars had their stereos playing loudly on top of the other sounds of the city.

I sat and watched for a while. The boy was very quick for a mortal and if a person was looking for him from the ground level, they may not have noticed him sitting in the shadows. There was also a male watching him from up the street but I couldn't get a good look at him because he was partially hidden by the fences and the porch roofs between us.

There was something unsettling about the whole situation. It felt like there were cold fingers walking up my spine and my fangs started to come out involuntarily. I didn't think about it much at the time and chalked it up to anxiety.

I waited until there was a break in cars pulling up. The last car in the line was a buyer so the boy had come out of his hiding spot and turned his back to me to hide once again. I jumped off the roof and landed only a few feet behind him. He started to turn around but I grabbed him by the back of his neck and pinned him against the wall. I kicked his left leg so that he was in the typical "spread 'em" position that cops use but instead of his hands supporting him against the wall, it was his head. I rifled through his pockets and found his stack of cash.

The boy yelled "Hey" to his buddy up the street, but it came out muffled because half of his face was against the wall. Then he yelled loud enough so that his teenaged voice squeaked. The man up the street pulled his gun out of the small of his back and started jogging at us. As he pointed his gun at me, I leapt to a nearby roof and ran off before he had time to squeeze the trigger.

When I got home I counted the cash, I had made about $1300. It was enough to cover rent but not much more.

CHAPTER 7

After three months I still hadn't told anyone what I was. I went from constantly instant messaging and e-mailing my friends during the day to not having any contact with them. I told people that I was super busy but that begins to fall apart. People assumed that I was mad at them or that I didn't want to be friends anymore but that couldn't have been farther from the truth. I missed my friends more than they will ever know, but I didn't know how to overcome the growing chasm between the day-timers and myself. Besides, what would we have talked about? They would've told me about their jobs and I didn't have one. I couldn't tell them how I killed people for dinner. The hardest part was that my physical appearance had changed. I was so pale that I looked like I had spent the past few months in a cave, and there was no hiding the fact that I had the eyes of a predator.

Andrew came home from work one day and before he could go upstairs, I called him into my English basement, saying that we needed to talk. Andrew was still wearing his suit and tie. When he came in, he couldn't help but look around because he owned it. I used to think that he was judging me but now I'm pretty sure that he was curious about how well his friend was taking care of his overpriced house. On the other hand, his wife Anne was definitely judging me.

"Oh Christ," he said. "Are you moving out?"

"What?" I said, "No. Not at all. It's bigger than that."

"You are gay! I knew it."

"Don't you wish, you little boom boom boy," I said. "You have been looking to mount me for years. Your wife is going to be so sad."

"So what's up?" His wife knew that he was downstairs and he works long hours so his time is short on weekdays.

"I'm not really sure how to say this. You know how I'm all pale and I've changed jobs? Well…"

Then I flashed the fangs at him. I tried to have a blank look on my face in an effort to not be intimidating, but he still jumped a little bit. He stood up a little straighter to hide that fact that I had scared the shit out of him. He wasn't aware how scared of me he was, but I heard his heart rate increase. He leaned forward and squinted his eyes trying to get a better look at my fangs.

"Those aren't real," he paused to look again, "are they?"

He was caught in the hinterland between primal fear and fascination.

"Look at me. I look like death warmed over. I am death warmed over. You can try to relax. I'm not dangerous, obviously."

"When did this happen?" he said. "Do you have to eat people? You look like shit. Anne thinks you are on drugs. "

"No. I don't eat people. Gross. I'm not a zombie."

I put my arms out like a walking zombie and growled, "mmmrrrrrrmmmm" while walking towards him.

"Christ, that's disturbing. Let's not do that." Then he laughed nervously.

"I don't eat people. I drink blood."

Then without thinking about it I ran my tongue over my fangs. Then I realized that they were still out and I retracted them. For a moment, my vampire instincts made me want to take a little bit of the blood that he had running through his veins. It was hard to resist when I could hear his heart thump. Fortunately he happened to be avoiding eye contact with me and didn't see me staring at his neck.

"Oh, yeah. That's better. Blood." He shook his head smiling a little bit. "Have you been out there rampaging around and killing people?"

"No, well, yes. But only super sick people," I said. "And it doesn't hurt them. It's a relief for them."

"Like Dr. Kevorkian?"

"Yeah. Sort of. But without the creepy van. He had a van right?" I wasn't trying to get off topic, I was genuinely curious.

"Maybe. I don't know." Andrew shook his head to get rid of the van question. "How did this happen?"

"I don't know. I'm still trying to figure it out. The last thing I can remember is being wasted at The Pour House. Then when I woke up I was like this."

"How do you know that you are a vampire then?"

"I like to drink blood, I'm basically Superman and the sun is my Kryptonite. Ring any bells?"

"Superman? You're like Superman?"

"Come outside and I'll show you."

We went outside and down the steps to the sidewalk. The night was cold and clear. There were patches of dirty, compacted snow on the ground.

"Have you ever seen anyone jump to the top of a house?" I said.

Then I sprinted to the other side of the street and leapt to the top of a three-story house. I tried not to land too hard because I knew the people who lived underneath were home. I heard someone in the house say something about wine on my way up. When I landed it was quiet in the house. I assumed that they were looking up and wondering what the hell was happening on their roof. I waved at Andrew and did a Flatley-esque jig. Then I jumped down and landed a few feet away from him.

"Holy shit." He looked at me, then the roof, then back at me

"Holy shit is right."

He stood there staring at the distance between the house and us. I turned and started to walk back towards the house when his wife came out.

"What are you guys doing?" Anne asked with a little suspicion.

"Nothing." I said. "I just wanted to show him something that is wrong with my car. Of course he has no idea how to fix it."

She looked back and forth between the two of us. She knew that I was lying but she didn't want to get involved.

"Oh well," I said. "All right, I'll talk to you guys later."

Then I went down the steps to my place and he went upstairs with his wife. He glanced back at me like he was going to say something but then thought better of it and went inside.

I felt a little better now that my secret was off of my chest. I trusted Andrew not to tell anyone for a while. Unfortunately, secrets have a way about coming out in DC. Just ask Nixon or Clinton.

"Hey stranger."

I didn't want to turn around, because if I didn't then she wouldn't be there. I knew that no matter how much I hoped she wouldn't be there, Charlie was back. She had made me into a vampire orphan and I hadn't forgiven her. When I did turn around, much to my embarrassment, I wanted to cry. If she had only given me a little bit of her time, the last two months would have been much easier. I know it sounds dramatic and I'm not Oliver fucking Twist but come on.

I didn't know what to say so I stood there in silence.

"Awwww. I've never seen something that is supposed to be a nightmare look so sad." Then she mocked me by pouting.

She came over and gave me a hug. I wish I could say that I pushed her away and told her what a bitch she was but it was my first physical contact since I had turned. She felt small with her head on my chest and I felt comforted.

She pulled back from me so she could see my face. She reached up with her hand and wiped my face. "Honey, you can't bleed tears in public, okay?"

I nodded.

We strolled through Chinatown, holding hands like a regular couple. I tried to absorb everything that was going on but it was impossible to look around when there were so many people on a small sidewalk. The second I quit paying attention to the people in front of me to look at all of the flashing neon signs, I would almost run into someone.

"Are you going to talk or hold my hand in silence all night?" She asked.

I waited a few steps.

"Yeah, I guess." I said.

"You're still alive. That is quite a feat." Then she smiled.

"Sometimes I forget that I'm a pawn in Charlie's game of life," I said.

"Yes! A pawn. That's more descriptive. I've been thinking of you as my little vamp cub but you are much larger than I am, so it didn't really fit."

"Thanks for the fucking help."

"You're relatively smart for a boy. Isn't it better knowing that you can survive on your own?"

"You mean isn't it better to feel alone? To feel completely lost and not even know how to feed myself?"

"Oh yeah. Leanne Washington," she said a little too loudly.

I looked around to see if anyone heard her.

"Yep, that was me."

"Wow. My savage boy."

I relaxed a little. It was nice to be able to get the weight of the killing off of my shoulders to someone who understood my circumstances. I had recently told Andrew that I was a vamp but he couldn't possibly understand what happened with Leanne Washington. Andrew couldn't understand that my natural instincts took over. My mortal friends don't even get hungry unless they skip lunch because of work. If I explained it to Andrew he would be okay at first, but then he would start wondering if he or his wife was next. From there his thoughts about his safety would spiral out of control. I knew that if I had been a little hungrier and one of them had been around it would have been curtains for someone.

"Yeah," I said, "it was pretty awful. If you would've taught me how to feed then it wouldn't have been like that."

"But the first time is so exciting. I didn't want to rob you of it. How did you do it?" When she asked her pupils dilated a little and she became excited.

"I yanked her into an alley and drained her. I was about as subtle as a bear attack. Then I puked when it was over."

"That happens," she said as she nodded. "I think it is psychological."

"It was pretty nasty."

Then we walked for a little while in silence until she pulled me into an upscale bar by the Spy Museum. We pushed our way through the crush of the crowd that was mingling near the bar but not actively getting drinks. Charlie got through the crowd first and ordered us two gin and tonics. It took me a minute to figure out that we stood out as it was and people slowly dissipated away from us. If you were to ask them why they moved away from us, they may not have noticed or they might have said that we were weird foreigners, but they had moved away from us like a herd of caribou from wolves. We held our drinks as camouflage and sat at a bar table for two.

"This is like a first date for us," she said.

"I don't really remember the night that we met."

"Oh. Was that you?" she said, acting like she was surprised. Then she rolled her eyes while making her best bimbo face and twirled her hair with her forefinger. I thought she was gorgeous and charming and I hated myself for it.

"So tell me anything about yourself?" I said. "Is Charlie even your real name?"

She wiggled, sat up straight and put her hands in her lap. She was mocking my serious tone but I blew it off.

"Yes. Charlie is what I go by," she said. "My name is Chantal-Genevieve Leglise."

"That's quite a mouthful."

"I was born in 1893. Before you hurt your pretty little head doing the math I'm 117, which makes me a super cougar. Or a Great GILF if I had children and so forth."

"You're really hot for being so old that Willard Scott could announce your birthday."

"Why thank you."

I smiled at her.

"I came to the U.S. with my family in 1909. My father died in an accident at work soon after, which was fairly common back then. We were living in New York City at the time, in Queens. When we got there it had just become part of the city. A few years later my mother got sick and died of consumption. They call it tuberculosis now but consumption is a better name for the disease. Not too long after that I was turned."

"By who?" I said.

"I have no idea what his name was. I was attacked after coming home late from work one night. He told me to have a nice life and I never saw him again."

"Is that why you turn people and then you don't help them because that is what happened to you?"

"Yes, and I have daddy issues too, Freud. Maybe that is why I did it at first but now it is just a litmus test. A few have survived but most don't."

"Where are the ones that have survived?"

"They've moved on from the city as years have passed."

"How many have you turned?"

"About 20 or so. More recently than before."

"Why?"

"I've been bored of my same old life. That is why I came down to DC. I was bored of the same old vampires. This life we live isn't an easy one. Everyone you have ever loved will die before you and you'll feel guilty because they won't continue on."

"Why didn't you turn your family members or friends or someone to keep you company?"

"It's against the rules," she said. "If I did it would be the death penalty for me and whomever I turn. It has to be that way or we would turn all of our family and friends.

Eventually who we are would get out and that would be the end of us."

"Okay."

"Enough personal questions. What else do you need to know?"

"Well," I said. "What else do I need to know?"

"Basically three things. Don't get caught in the sun. We are super allergic or something to silver, so if it touches our skin then it burns and basically takes away all of our strength so avoid silver handcuffs in your weird sex games. And we can't go into people's houses or places of worship without being invited."

"I don't play kinky sex games. Jesus. We can't go into people's houses without being invited? That's strange."

"Yeah, some vamps think it is proof of God, and others think it is to prevent us from being able to kill at will."

"What do you think?"

"I flip-flop back and forth. It depends on what kind of mood I'm in."

"I know the feeling."

"How old are you?"

"27."

"I figured. It is good to get turned in your 20s because then you look about as good as you ever will for the rest of eternity. It's sad when people are turned in their 60s or something. They are perennially old."

We sat for a few more minutes.

"Can we leave?" she asked. "I don't feel like being here any more and I'm hungry."

"Of course."

When we got outside I asked her if I could go feed with her and she said, "No. We generally don't feed together because it can create too much blood lust and things can get out of hand. I'm a lady, you don't want to watch me feed."

"I really do though."

"Goodnight."

"Goodnight."

As I walked away I looked into the passenger side rear-view mirror of a car parked on the street and I saw her watching me.

Andrew called me a few minutes after sunset because he wanted to meet for a beer or two. We met in the basement of one of the many dive bars that line the Capitol Hill end of Pennsylvania Avenue. The sign above the stairs that descended into the basement said "Losers" with an arrow pointing down. Downstairs there was a small bar and some flat screen TVs against the wall. The place had the dank smell of a bar that has served fried food for the last thirty years. It wasn't a first date kind of bar. It was the bar people would go to meet up with their booty calls at 1:00am.

I saw Andrew at one of the tables. I greeted the bearded bartender and he poured me an Arrogant Bastard ale without asking what I wanted. It wasn't an arraignment of my character. He knew it is my favorite beer.

"Hey, how's work?"

"Fine," he said. He was distracted and only making occasional eye contact. "It doesn't really matter. I haven't been able to get any work done knowing that I have an immortal creature of the night living right below me."

"When you say it like that it sounds pretty awful," I said.

"I mean, it isn't as if I should be afraid of you. Right?"

He punctuated his sentence by looking at me with genuine concern and that hurt my feelings or what was left of them. I had learned to stuff down a lot of emotions when my very existence depended on killing other living things, but then again any human's continued existence depends on something else dying. People eat cows, chickens and eggs all the time. I suck the blood out of people who are dying anyway, that doesn't make me a monster. It made me sound like a monster though. I'm sure some cannibal would agree with my logic.

"No, of course not," I said, lowering my voice to a whisper. "You don't need to be afraid of me. I only take people who are deathly ill. I can see it in their eyes and hear it in their breath and heartbeat. I'm not rampaging around killing people."

"But you're killing people," he said.

"Yeah. You're right. But most of them see me as a relief. A couple of them have even thanked me." This was a bit of a stretch intended to drive home my point. "I talk to them and try to offer them comfort. I can drain people that weak before they even realize what is going on. Do you think it is a good idea for people to linger connected to machines for days or months? It is inhumane and a tremendous drain on society. Some people hang on by a little thread for so long that their families are relieved when they die. I don't feel guilty about this. If given the chance, I bet some of the families who are mourning would thank me as well."

"I understand the point of euthanizing people. But you are doing it yourself. There is a big difference between having a doctor pull the plug on someone and you coming in to do whatever the hell it is that you do. You're making the decision for them."

I watched the bubbles in my beer float to the top. Until that point I had assumed that every person in the hospice had wanted to die at least on some level. That's why a person ends up in the hospice, to die.

"Did you have anything to do with Leanne Washington?"

I had hoped that he wouldn't ask me about her.

"No. I'm not sure what that was all about or even if it was one of us."

"Us?" He said.

"Well, yeah. I think that is the proper word at this point. There are you guys and then there's us."

"The predators and the prey you mean?"

"I don't think of it like that at all. That's way too morbid. We exist at night and you guys mainly exist during the day. It's like we live on two different planets."

We sat there and watched a college basketball game for a bit but not a word passed between us. When he finished his beer he got up.

"Alright man. I'll catch you later then."

"Yeah," I said, "It was good to see you for once."

We shook hands out of habit and when he grabbed mine he looked down repulsed at how cold it was. It made me feel bad but I couldn't blame him. Then he paid our tab at the bar and left.

CHAPTER 8

I decided to go back and rob the drug dealer again because I needed rent money. They couldn't call the cops on me. I put on my all black hoodie and some jeans and left the house. On my way over, I felt bad for the little fellow that I was going to rob again. I had hoped that he didn't get beaten by his dealer or something for losing the money. Unfortunately for him, he was about to lose more and he didn't have a choice in the matter.

I sat on the roof and had the feeling that someone had just walked across my grave. My fangs popped out and I saw a young, black male was standing on the roof near me. He scared the shit out of me because I knew he was one of my own. He was wearing an impeccable black suit with a blue shirt and a matching tie that was the same color as his eyes.

"Well hello," he said. "I've heard that you are giving my men a bit of trouble." He had a slight British accent that made him sound intelligent. His hello came out sounding more like the word yellow but without pronouncing the y.

"Only one of them," I said.

I was terrified but determined not to show it. Even though I'm dead, I wanted to keep living.

He smiled at me. He wasn't showing his fangs. Mine were out and I didn't know how to put them away. I felt like a mouse cornered by a cat.

"You must be new or you wouldn't be here," he said. "Where did you come from?"

"Uh," my voice cracked. "This girl named Charlie. Do you know her?"

"Yes." He shook his head with a look of distain, "I am aware of Charlie. How long have you been one of us?" The tone of his voice indicated that he clearly didn't think I was really part of the "us".

"Two months."

"She is a black widow spider. I am surprised you are alive. My name is John. What's your name?"

I finally had someone other than Charlie to talk about my new condition with. The questions tumbled around in my head.

"Stephen." Out of habit I wanted to shake hands but he didn't move towards me, and left me hanging. "Yeah, I'm surprised too. It isn't all that easy. She made me and didn't tell me shit about what to do or how to do it. I've had to sneak into shitty old hospitals to get blood from patients or feed off of stray animals."

He smiled at me. "That is quite disgusting."

"Yeah, no shit. And then when I asked her about what I'm supposed to do she kicked my ass, and then the second time I met up with her she wouldn't let me watch her feed so I could learn from her."

"We don't feed together because things tend to go off the rails so to speak. Then you decided to come steal from me?"

"I can't hold a job and I have to pay rent." I said. "And I didn't know that a vamp ran this, uh, deal here or I would've went elsewhere."

"How short are you this month?"

"$900."

He reached into his pocket and peeled off a wad of cash.

"This should cover it. Meet me here tomorrow and we can talk."

I didn't want to take the money but I didn't have a choice. "Are you sure?"

He waved me off with his hand. "Be here tomorrow and maybe I will teach you a thing or two about us."

I would say he was off like a puff of smoke but even smoke lingers for a second or two. He didn't.

The next day I showed up with the same black sweatshirt with the hood up, under it a black Baltimore Orioles hat and some dark blue jeans. I didn't want to stand out in the neighborhood so I made my face hard to see. For a short time I considered not showing up but I didn't want to start shit with the only other vampire that I knew, aside from Charlie.

I walked to the corner where I had robbed the boy a month or so before and he was sitting on the stairs outside of the same gutted row house. As soon as he saw me he stood up. He let his fight or flight instincts work out their differences very slowly. To his credit he stayed. Then, without saying a word, he pointed down the street. I turned my head slowly to look because I was wondering if he was going to pull the old, "Hey look over there while I hit you in the noggin with this brick" routine.

John pulled up in an eggshell-white SUV that must have cost a $100,000. I had never owned a vehicle that was so clean on the outside. Every light from the street bounced off of the paint after being magnified. He gave me a sideways head nod that told me to get in.

"If you were anyone else, I would run this device over you to see if you have a wire on you, but given your condition, I don't think I need to," John said holding up a metal detector.

"Of course not," I said. "When you have to kill people to survive, the police aren't really an option."

"That is true."

"So what's this all about? Why did you choose to help me? Please don't get me wrong, I'm grateful for it, I'm just curious."

He let out a deep breath. "It is funny to me. I've found that people are more likely to question my motives when I'm being kind than when I'm being mean. I guess when people are mean, other people think that is just the way they are but when someone is nice, people wonder what they really want."

I nodded and wondered where he was going with this.

"I helped you because you are one of us now. I am not saying that being one of us is like being a part of a team where everyone looks out for each other. We operate almost exclusively on our own but when someone is new and they are engaging in risky behavior or endangering our livelihoods then the appropriate steps need to be taken. When one of us is in a desperate situation it is our duty to help them out because we cannot risk exposure."

"How many of us are there?"

"Some. Less than you would think. We have a cap on how many can live in an area, depending on the population. It is kind of like your House of Representatives. But unlike them we keep a cap on it, because if there are too may of us then we will decimate the population. Do not bother seeking them out. They know of your existence and the fact that Charlie is threatening our way of life. If any of them want to speak to you, they will."

"Okay." I said. "I'll keep on keeping on I guess."

"Yes. You do that. In the mean time I have a proposition."

"Okay. I'm in. Wait, does it pay?" I was so eager to have something to do. Anything was better than nothing.

"Yes, it pays. Do you care to know what you will be doing?"

"Of course."

"I need you to run security for a few weeks on weekends. Once you work off the money that you stole from me, I will start paying you. The amount you receive will depend on how much we sell. You won't have any contact with my men. If any of them get caught they can't know about your existence. Who knows what they would say if they were if they were facing jail time. We know that authorities wouldn't ever believe a criminal if they were talking about super-human powers, but there is no reason to risk it. If something happens, you will need to minimize your show of force in public, or people are going to talk. The boy that you robbed told people that you were like a comic book character. I had to convince him that he had hit his head during the struggle with you and had misperceived your abilities."

"When do I start?"

"Tomorrow night. Midnight. Watch the guys from the same roof we met on. Okay?"

"Okay."

The next night and the following weekends I was John's eyes and ears, his one-man security team, but nothing happened.

The first night I was ready to fight off a horde of thieves and con men, but people weren't that brave. There were a few junkies who got a little aggressive with the guys who were holding but it wasn't anything that they hadn't seen before. Mainly they had to deal with empty promises from people who wanted to get a little bit now and pay them back later.

After paying John back, I had made a few hundred dollars in the course of a weekend, which wasn't all that much but more than I was bringing in otherwise. It gave me something to do with my nights now that I was completely alienated from everyone that I knew.

I sat on the roof and read the Hannibal series by Thomas Harris and some other books. I actually enjoyed myself for the first time in a long time. I think being around people was good for me, even though they didn't know I was there.

After feeding on a house cat (it tasted a little fishy), I went back to the church that I had thrown the cross off of. I jumped to the lowest part of the roof and climbed to the top. I had a pretty good vantage point from up there. After looking around for a while I sat in the dark with my back to the steeple so that no one would be able to see me even without the missing cross.

The pastor was preaching a sermon from the Bible, more specifically, the Book of Job. For the uninitiated the story is about God's faithful worshipper Job, who according to the Bible, "He was the greatest man among all the people of the East."

The story is basically a cosmic test of Job's faith. God allows the Devil to kill all of Job's ten offspring, make him poor and give him boils. It is supposed to inspire faith in God even in the face of adversity, because no matter what a parishioner is going through it couldn't be as bad as what Job went through. Job remained pious through all of his misfortune and so should the congregants.

I waited on the steeple until everyone had left but the pastor. I heard the pastor's wife tell him that she would see him at home. He puttered around in the chapel and then walked the length of the middle of the church and locked the front doors.

I slid down the roof and ran to the front door. Even though he had locked the door a few seconds before I started to pull on the door very slowly to see if I could yank it open. It wouldn't budge so I knocked.

He opened the door. "What can I help you with my son?"

"I need a little advice," I said.

He sighed under his breath. I could tell that he wanted to go home but his pastoral instincts didn't allow him to tell people to get lost. He stood next to the door and nodded for me to come in.

"May I come in?"

A look of confusion flashed over his face because he had opened the door and gave me every indication that I could come in but I still asked anyway. Then his pupils dilated.

"Sure. Come on in." His eyes focused on me. He knew what I was.

I don't know what would've happened to me without the invitation, but it had been made clear that I couldn't go into domiciles or churches without being invited. I guess hospices, hospitals, and hotels don't count with the invitation rule because people (and God or gods) don't stay there permanently.

"What seems to be the matter?" he said. I showed him my fangs but he didn't flinch, which made me wonder if he had met a vampire before.

"Your sermon is what is the matter," I said. "It was a pile of shit. I don't mean your delivery because you really sold the hell out of it." I smiled at my own cleverness while showing my fangs in all their evil glory. "God allows the Devil to kill Job's children and that is supposed to inspire faith? Job's children are the sacrificial lambs of some bet between heaven and hell. It seems like a raw deal to me."

He clasped his hands together in front of him in a gentle way that I was supposed to make me feel calm. It didn't.

"I don't know the fate of Job's children once they died but I'm sure they were given special consideration for their sacrifice. And we don't allow cursing in our church."

If his voice had been patronizing in anyway I would have drained him on the spot, but he was controlled and stated his opinion like fact.

"Perhaps if you are going to preach about how your flock should remain faithful in the face of adversity, we should find an interesting way to test you."

For the first time he showed genuine emotion. His face went pale. "I believe that in the course of one's life, a person is tested many, many times."

"Oh, we aren't talking about other people. We are talking about you and I'm here now."

"How long have you been like this, my son?"

"I'm not your son and what does it matter?" I said.

"I'm just curious. You came here for a reason. What is it? Are you here to take my life?"

"If I wanted to kill you, you would be dead already. Does that scare you? Are you certain that you would go to heaven?"

"I only fear the pain that you would cause me and the hurt that my family would feel, not death. Death is the end. No more pain."

"Then off to heaven you go?"

"I hope so but one never really knows, do they?"

"I guess not." I said. Then I walked to the front of the church and looked at all the pews. I walked up the five steps and stood at the podium. I felt like I could be a pastor. I could then control my minions of vampires and slowly take over the world. "You must feel pretty special to be able to stand up here week after week and tell people what to think."

"The Lord keeps me humble. It isn't my words, it is the word of God."

"Where is your God now?" I said. I grabbed him by his shoulders. I held him tight while talking to his neck in a whisper. "He can't save you when you need him the most."

His breath was shaky as he tried to calm himself. "No, you are wrong. God is always here." Then he took a deep breath. "You aren't welcome here anymore demon. Leave now."

I shot out the front door like I had been fired out of a cannon, rolling into the street. I was lucky there weren't any cars coming or I would've been hit. I couldn't have been more shocked.

Part of me wanted to wait until he left and kill him, but I figured that I was still new being a vampire, and he knew a thing or two more about this than I did. I had already planned on coming back. Besides, he had to leave the church sometime.

CHAPTER 9

I decided to go to New York City because I needed to get away from DC. I had Andrew watch Diablo for the night and left. All of the changes that I had gone through in past few months were a significant weight and I thought a trip would help unload the burden. While I was driving up there I wasn't sure how I was going to pay for it. The hotel cut pretty deep into my bank account. I had decided beforehand that if I was going to go to NYC then I was going to stay in Times Square. At least I wouldn't have to worry about feeding, because I took care of it before I left. My goal was to absorb the city with my vampire senses. If I wanted to save money, I would have stayed in Newark or somewhere else. I figured that I would take more security shifts for John when I got home to cover the costs.

My $375 (tax not included) room was smaller than the average American's bedroom. I had planned on staying a few nights but I could only afford to stay one.

I had packed all black so that everything matches and black is the only color that blood doesn't stain.

I rode the elevator from the 37th floor to the lobby. Long elevator rides have always made me queasy. There was motion going on around me but I wasn't moving at all. The elevator doors opened to reveal a packed lobby. Families that were waiting to get checked in had taken all of the lounge chairs so I didn't have a middle ground to relax in before I went out into the city. The set of glass automatic doors at the front of the hotel was constantly opening and closing, letting in the roar of the city and then muting it, over and over again.

Without another option I ventured out of the hotel into the madness. I was already rethinking the decision to come to NYC. DC was a quiet little town compared to Times Square. There were so many cabs lined up that the cars looked more like an enormous centipede than individual vehicles.

The light from the billboards was so bright it created shadows upon shadows. I couldn't tell where one shadow ended and another began. It was as close to being in the sun as I would ever get. The light gave off a bit of warmth to people walking by. Subconsciously or not, they walked closer to the wall to be closer to the signs, like little consumer moths.

I was only a few blocks south on 7th Avenue from my hotel when my fangs came out. Fortunately, I'm sure that no one noticed because they were too busy looking around so I retracted them. I knew that it meant that there was a vamp in the vicinity but I wasn't able to figure out who it was. There were at least 25,000 people on the street in a four-block radius.

There's a sidewalk in the middle of the street that separates Broadway and 7th before they merge and that's where I was standing when a young man who appeared to be a meth addict approached me. He smelled like Brie that had been in the sun for too long.

"What are you doing here?" he asked me.

"I'm a tourist, here to take a look around. That's all." I replied. While I was responding he walked a circle around me, checking me out. I didn't move. His vampy essence radiated off of him.

"Allow me to be more clear. Are you here to hunt? Because you look young and I can tell by your posture that you haven't been here before." He said. He had stopped circling me and now he was standing really close to me. He moved like a snake. Anyone who was watching him would know that he was a predator. They may not know what kind of predator, but he was clearly dangerous. He might as well have been shaking a rattle like a snake.

"No. I'm not here to hunt. Just one night to visit."

"You aren't with anyone. Why are you here?"

"I needed to get away for a little bit, okay?" I said. He snake-iness and smell was getting on my nerves. I started to walk away.

He appeared in front of me and two guys started watching us that I hadn't noticed before. One of the guys had a black leather coat on and a Yankees cap, while the other had long brown hair past his shoulders and faded jeans. He looked like Alice In Chains guitarist Jerry Cantrell.

"Get away from what? We don't want trouble here. This is where we've lived for decades, this is our home." The other two guys had flanked me.

"I'm trying to relax."

"You decided to relax in one of the busiest places on earth?"

"Yeah. I guess. I clearly didn't think this through."

"No you didn't."

Then a cop came up.

"Is there a problem here guys? Are you harassing a tourist?" said the cop.

"No sir," said the snaky leader.

"Good. Move along then," he said.

They walked off without giving me another look. The cop looked at me.

"Sorry about that. Some New Yorkers think that they own the place. Not all of us are assholes, that's just the rumor."

"It's cool," I said. "I wasn't scared or anything."

"Yeah right," he said looked amused at my obvious lie. "The next time you are here, don't stare at the billboards so much. The locals never bother to look at them. When you look at them it lets all the scumbags in the area know that you are a mark."

"Okay. Thanks," I said.

"Have a good night." Then he walked off.

I went back to the hotel. I didn't want to run back into those guys again. I made up a story to the front desk that my room was too small and the sheets were too dirty. I threatened to start yelling about how there were bedbugs in my room and the manager looked around his packed lobby and promptly refunded my money. I got in my car and left. The sun was going to come out soon so I stayed at a chain hotel off of I-95 for the night. My plan had failed to distract me. My own kind didn't want me. I felt alone more than ever.

I went back to the hospice. It had been a little while since my last visit. I figured it was okay to visit once or twice a month but anything more and I might have raised some suspicions. I found an unlocked window on the second floor and held onto the sill with one hand while slowly opening the window with the other. It was the same room that I had visited the first time but now there was a new patient. I let myself through the window and stood there for a moment watching the woman sleep.

"You've come for me," she said. "It is about time. I've been waiting for you."

"You have?" I responded. I'm a little ashamed to admit that this old and dying woman startled me.

"Of course I have. Who else would I be expecting?" she said. "I've seen you here before. It's okay. I'm not going to tell anyone. And who would believe an old lady like me anyway."

She smiled softly at me. Her big brown eyes put me at ease. She was the every mom. All at once I knew that she could heal a skinned knee and not take any sass while cooking with two pots on the stove and a dish in the oven.

"Who would have thought Death was an average-looking white guy?" she said to herself.

"Average-looking? Ouch." I said with a smile. "We come in all shapes and sizes and you just happen to be in my jurisdiction."

I was making up my alibi as being Death on the fly. In the back of my mind I wondered if other people had seen me come and go.

"Well that's fine with me. You seem pleasant enough."

"You've noticed me before?" I said.

"Twice. And both times people died in the night. Will it hurt?"

"I don't think so. But I haven't ever experienced death myself so I can't be sure."

"Okay. I guess we will see then. Where are you from?"

I wasn't used to someone else being in control of the conversation or even having people be awake. I could've taken her by force but that didn't feel right. I had been lonely for a while.

"I'm from Alaska." I said. I wasn't sure why I told her that piece of the truth at the time but now I know that I didn't want to keep lying to a woman that I was about to kill. To this day I don't know why I held on to a sense of morality at that moment.

"That's exciting. My Death is from Alaska. I've always wanted to visit Alaska. It looks so pretty. Wide open air and big, beautiful mountains." She closed her eyes. "I can see it now in my head."

I was tempted to take her right then but she looked so pleasant that I didn't.

"Have you travelled much?"

"No, not much. I've been to Virginia and Maryland but they don't really count. I've lived in DC for 82 years. The same house for 57 of them. I lived through the '68 riots and then the riot in 1991."

"The riots must have been scary."

"The '68 riots were because Martin Luther King, Jr. was killed. It felt like the whole world was going to crack in half and swallow itself. People burned houses down and when the firefighters came to put the fires out, people threw rocks and bottles at them. We were burning down our own neighborhood and not letting people help us save ourselves. It was the darnedest thing that I have ever seen. My husband Mack sat on the porch with his shotgun in his lap through the whole thing. He tried to make me stay inside but I would come out and talk to him and our neighbor Melvin until they would shoo me back inside. Melvin had his little Saturday Night Special peashooter in his lap like it could scare anyone. A man that big with a gun that small looks silly."

"How long did the riots last?"

"A few nights. People eventually ran out of alcohol and all stores in the neighborhood were closed, so people went back to work because rent was still due. Some people went to the same place that they were looting the day before. I don't understand those boys. If you want to break something, then you should at least have enough sense to leave your own neighborhood."

All of a sudden I didn't want to drink off of this woman. She was full of DC history that I hadn't heard before. She was so kind and thoughtful that I wanted to turn her so I could listen to her stories.

"You've lived through two sets of riots?" I said.

"Oh yes. The other one was in 1991. It was a little north of where I lived in Mount Pleasant. It sure wasn't pleasant during that time. Ha. That's a joke." Then she smiled in a big, broad way that made the world feel like a better place to live in. "A woman cop, if I remember correctly, shot a Mexican during some celebration. People were burning police cars and buses. They said that the police were mistreating the Mexicans in DC, but they were DC police; they mistreated everyone who wasn't rich and white. If you were poor and white, they would rough you up as well as they would a black man or a Mexican. They were equal opportunity with their nightsticks if you were poor. Instead of taking you in for jail time, they used to beat people up and tell them if they ever did it again that they would beat them up worse. That usually worked."

Out of habit, I looked at my watch. I still had an hour before I would need to leave. The lady smiled at me.

"I hope I'm not taking up too much of your time. No one wants to listen to an old lady ramble on and on."

"No, no, go on. Please," I said, "I don't get to talk to people very often. Tell me about your husband."

She looked sad on my behalf.

"Mack? He died a couple years back from a heart attack. We were married for 50 years on the button. Some times I think that he held out from dying so we could make it to our 50-year anniversary. He had a couple of strokes before the heart attack and I think he wanted to have one last party with our family."

While she was talked, she looked out the window like I wasn't even there. She was a woman who realized that her turn on the merry-go-round of life was about over.

"Do you have kids?" I kept asking her questions so she wouldn't turn the subject back to me.

"We had three children, Alton, Charles and James. Mack wanted to have a girl so he could have a Daddy's Little Girl but it wasn't in the cards. He blamed me and I blamed him, but it was all in fun. Alton is a professor at Howard University. He helps kids become social workers. Charles works construction and James, he died in a car crash when he was 17. I thought his death was going to kill me and it made a pretty good run at it. I've never got quite over James dying, but I suppose a parent never does. I kept on living my life. Every day it got a little easier. Do you have a family?"

I didn't want to talk about myself but I also didn't see the harm in it. She was going to die anyway.

"I had a family," I said. "Not so much any more. There is a lot of time and space between us if you get my drift."

"Do you come from a whole family of Deaths or is it just you?"

"Just me."

"That must be very hard for you."

"I'm okay with it. It was hard at first but like you said, every day it gets a little easier."

"Not to be pushy, but are we going to start the death part soon, because I'm sleepy and I don't want to miss it."

I smiled at her, making sure that I didn't show my fangs.

"Not today." I said, "I think that we are going to have to wait until another day. Enjoy tomorrow's sunshine."

"So you will be back soon then?"

"I really don't know."

"Okay. But if you ever want to come back to talk, you are always welcome. I have to admit that it's nice knowing that Death isn't some scary boogeyman."

I started to leave and then I turned around.

"You should probably make sure you've said goodbye to your family. Just because I didn't do it doesn't mean that another Death won't be coming around."

"I will. Thank you," she said. "Goodnight."

Then she rolled over away from me and closed her eyes. It didn't take more than a minute until she was breathing heavily and having the small muscles spasms of the dreaming.

I climbed out the window, still hungry but feeling a little better about myself.

CHAPTER 10

Wandering the streets, I'd come to realize the frailty of human life. When I walked past people, they had no idea how close they were passing to death. It wasn't some far-off metaphor that they wouldn't have been able to understand. It was me, and it really wouldn't take much to show them. Some times I wanted them to recognize my power but it was counter-intuitive to keeping my condition a secret.

Before I turned I spent most of my waking hours concerned about money. I never had much growing up so I thought that once I got older I would have a nice watch and drive a nice car like people on television. But now that I was responsible for taking people's lives, I didn't really care about having possessions any more. I only cared about my continued existence.

When I saw people blowing money on $100,000 cars it made me ashamed that I used to want one. I mean, to each his own, and if a person makes it then they have the right to spend it any way they want to, but they must know that it would be better spent elsewhere like on educating children or feeding those in need.

It was hard for me to even talk about material possessions because growing up with a widowed mother taught my brother and me to lower our expectations. Out of anger I started keying expensive cars with my nails (or is it nailing?). If I saw an expensive brand-new car, I would dig one of my nails into the side of the car and keep walking. When I finished I would pull the paint out of my nails and smile to myself. I'm not delusional enough to think that this would change anyone's behavior but it felt good. I was a vampire so I didn't have to worry about getting caught. The only people who could've caught me were my own kind.

One night I was walking along scraping a few layers of paint off of a grey Mercedes Benz AMG when I saw a homeless man peering out of an alley 20 feet away from me. The sound of the scraping metal had drowned out all the other sounds in the vicinity and I hadn't noticed him.

As soon as he noticed that I saw him, he turned tail down the alley screaming, "There's another, there's another, there's another…" on repeat.

My instincts took over. He was running away and advertising my existence to everyone in his vocal range so I had to stop him.

Afterward, when I thought about it, I was sure that no one would've believed him that I was a vampire or whatever he thought I was, but I was so startled at the time I couldn't take the chance.

I came around the corner and he was making a gimpy break for the next street over. I ran after him but then I decided to add a bit of flair to my attack. I said, "Hey!" and before he had time to turn around I leapt to a ledge on building to my left. From the ledge I pushed off of the wall towards him. By the time he fully turned around, I plowed into him like a professional wrestler jumping off of the top rope. My stomach hit his chest, our bodies making a perfect "T".

I was around three stories high at my peak and when we collided I felt his ribs snap. I got up and yelled, "That's for all my little Hulkamaniacs!" and I strutted around with my hand in the air like I was holding the World Wrestling Championship Belt while I imitated the sound of the crowd going wild with my other hand over my mouth.

It took me a minute to realize that I wasn't really celebrating a victory and that the man was barely conscious and in pain. As I drank his blood I felt bad for hurting the poor guy.

My mom told me not to play with my food and I'm sure that included this situation.

I felt bad after attacking the homeless man. I knew that I should've shown more compassion but I didn't. Plain and simple. I was struggling not to lose my grip on humanity and I needed someone who could understand what I was going through. Part of me thought that eventually it wouldn't matter that I was killing people. I cared the first twenty times or so but after the 100th person it wouldn't matter. On a long enough time, no matter how shocking it was, the distress and guilt would go away.

The last time I had hung out with Charlie, the conversation was good and getting to talk to another vamp helped ease my mind. It was easy to understand that either I have to kill someone to live or I will die myself, but that doesn't make it any easier. Perhaps I didn't need to drain people fully to stay alive, but then I would have to feed more often.

I could've talked to John about my conundrum but I would've rather talked to Charlie.

I decided it was time to go back to the church. I wanted to turn it up a notch on them and maybe get some money as well. I could always use the extra cash. Maybe I would go straight monster on them and tear up the place. I didn't have any plan in particular. Only the pastor had seen me, so now I would scare the whole congregation. All I needed was to get someone to invite me in and I would cause as much damage as I could before the pastor evicted me again.

The prospect of reigning terror on the congregation excited me. It isn't that I hated the pastor or anyone else at his church. It was a mere test of their faith, like the story of Job. If they wanted to be let into God's kingdom then they had to be willing to walk through some fire, so to speak.

I waited until there was a packed house and swung down from the top of the steeple. I was about to try to kick in the double doors and yell, "I am Satan!" when a set of seemingly frail arms wrapped around me and all of a sudden I was airborne. I tried to peel the arms off but they were harder than steel. I couldn't get them to budge.

We landed at short time later in the corner of a park that had most of the lights busted out. Before we landed I was let go. My forward momentum propelled me to do a couple somersaults until a bush graciously stopped me. I got up and brushed myself off.

Standing there was a pencil-thin, black man in his 60s wearing a gray, summer-weight three-piece suit. His cane was an ivory swan connected to dark black stained wood with a silver tip at the bottom. For a man with a cane, he didn't have a problem with speed.

"My name is Simon," he said. "I apologize for your rough landing. I thought you were going to land on your feet." He spoke with a mild Irish accent that only came out when he was pronouncing his Rs.

He held his cane horizontally in front of him, ready for battle. I held both of my hands open at my sides.

"Hey, it's cool." I said, "There's no reason for us to get into it. I have no problems with you." Ninety-five percent of the time you hear someone say that, it is because they don't want to get their butt kicked. This was definitely one of those times.

"I'm glad to hear that. Now what is the meaning of this nonsense with the church?" He put his cane down and began to lean on it a little.

"I don't know. I mean," I said, losing my confidence. "I walk by that church all the time and I'm sick of hearing his crap. He is promising people an afterlife in exchange for 10% of their wages. If they really do believe in God then what would it matter if I rattled their faith a little bit?" I felt like a child who had been asked by his father why had he done something dumb.

"I understand. John went through a phase like yours but it was 200 years ago. Listen to me closely. There are too many people with cell phone cameras for you to be acting like a fool. You would have enjoyed the 1700s, the world was a much larger place. But now, if you act like you are a living, breathing demon, the whole world will know. Whether you understand or not, your actions could threaten our very existence and we cannot allow that. Do you understand what I mean?"

"Yeah, I understand."

"It is better for us to let them live their lives in religious worlds."

"It's a bunch of shit though."

"You are the first new vampire in this area in over 100 years and you have already figured out whether or not God exists?" He didn't sound condescending or mean when he asked, even though it would have been justified.

He waited for me to answer but I didn't have a retort.

"Do you ever think that maybe God, or whatever is responsible for our change, made rules so that we can't enter someone's house without an invitation on purpose so we won't be able to do whatever we want? So that people would be able to feel safe at home and their house of worship? In case you are curious, we can't go into mosques, temples, or synagogues either without being invited. Also, every holy man that I have ever met knows if they tell us that we are uninvited, we have to leave their church. That part works pretty well, doesn't it?"

"Yeah, a little too well. I didn't see that coming." I smiled and shook my head. Now that he admitted to knowing that I was a jackass I was able to relax a little in his presence.

"I know that you did not ask to be brought into this." he said. "But we have a peaceful existence here and we don't want to mess it up. I understand your feelings regarding churches, this one in particular, but when you start problems eventually the Council has to deal with it and neither of us want that."

"Okay. I'll behave."

"We shall see." And then poof, he was gone before I could respond. Not once during my stay in DC was I able to get the last word in with other vamps.

CHAPTER 11

I sat in Dupont Circle and watched people roam around completely unaware that a monster was among them. The headlights and taillights of the cars speeding around the circle on a busy night felt like being in a blender with white and red Christmas tree lights. Then my fangs came out. I knew that it meant there was at least another vamp in the area, but like in New York City, there were too many people around for me to figure out who it was. From behind me came a voice.

"Hi."

And there was Charlie. She was wearing a black tank top with white letters that said, "Dear God, Fuck You". Which was a little over the top but I understood the sentiment. She was with this tall, lanky guy who couldn't have been a day over twenty. He was wearing a pink polo shirt over a yellow polo shirt and both collars were up. A typical Georgetown douchebag. I put my fangs away.

"Hello," I said to her. I nodded to him.

I didn't want the conversation to go any farther. I hoped she would keep walking. Her friend was looking around at the brilliance of the city. I could tell that he was a brand new vampire.

"Fangs!" she said, hitting her frat boy in the arm. He snapped out of his stupor and closed his eyes in concentration. It took him a second but he was able to put them away.

"I see you have a new friend," I said.

"Yeah, they come and they go," she said. "They mostly go. The eternal weakness of men I guess. If you put a few obstacles in front of them, they end up killing themselves or even worse, they make me do it for them."

This got the attention of the walking bag of douche.

"What do you mean?" he said.

"Quiet. We are talking now. I will talk to you later."

"I'm still here," I said.

"Yes, I'm aware of that." She said. Then she got distracted and turned around slowly, looking through the crowd. Mr. Two Polos and I both had our fangs come out again. This time it was much faster. I wasn't prepared and accidentally bit my lip.

And there he was, the cause of the commotion. Simon. He had on a dark grey wool coat and a matching newsboy hat. He looked even smaller than he did when he had stopped me at the church.

"We have spoken about you making vampires, Charlie. This is the last time. The Council does not want to be forced to take more drastic measures. We can't keep cleaning up after your messes."

"This is Simon," she said to Twin Polos and me. "He is a goon for The Council."

"Yeah," I said looking looking at him. "We've met."

Charlie looked at me. I could tell she was wondering what I was referring to.

"There are reasons behind our laws." he said. "You must obey them. We cannot let you keep creating vampires. We are over our maximum capacity by two right now so they must either leave our city or they must be taken care of. We will not risk exposure due to your need to behave like Medea. This is your last warning."

Then the old man strolled off down Connecticut Avenue. He had a slight limp and leaned heavily on his cane.

"Medea?" I wondered out loud.

"Yeah, the Greek lady who killed her children." Then Charlie smiled at the both of us. "His cane is a crock of shit."

"It looks like he uses it to me," I said, still thinking about Medea.

"If you ask anyone about it, they will tell you some story about a witch in Nigeria, but I think he uses it to trick people into thinking that he is a weakling."

"What does he mean that The Council says there are too many vampires?"

"Oh." she said with a sigh. "That old crap. There's a council in each region and they have a formula for how many of us can exist in a certain area and not risk exposure. The District couldn't support 500 vampires. There would be too many people dying and eventually the mortals would catch on. We have to eat once a week or so, which is around 50 people a year. Even though not all of us suck people. You're so gross."

I gave her the finger. She smiled.

"There used to be fifteen of us living here and now there are ten." She looked at the two of us. "Well, twelve. Because new technology, cameras, fingerprints and whatnot, The Council hasn't approved of making anyone in a long time. Lucky for you guys, I got bored and wanted some new friends."

"Yeah, really lucky. You're so sweet."

"Oh come on." she said standing closer to me, which caught the attention of her new boy toy. "You must love the power and immortality. If you don't, you will." Then she winked at me.

"Where are you guys off to tonight?" I said trying to change the subject.

"I don't know." she said. "I'm might throw him off a bridge or push him in front of a bus because I don't think he believes me that he is basically immortal."

"Typical first date," I said, shaking my head. "That's my cue to leave."

"Really?" She said. "I wish you would stay. We could have a lot of fun."

I wanted to stay and hang out with her but I didn't want to share her attention with anyone else.

"I have a date," I said. A weak attempt at making her jealous.

"You're a horrible liar but I appreciate the sentiment, my dear."

I smiled and walked away.

Even though I spent a majority of my time alone, there were some great moments, like when I snuck into RFK where the DC United professional soccer team plays. The goals were put away for the night but I brought one of them out with a ball and started playing by myself. The lights weren't on but I can see in the dark so it didn't matter much.

I started out kicking the ball from the mid-field line and aiming at the top post. I could hit it once out of every three or four times, but it was too close so I stood at the far end and kicked it from there. My aim wasn't very good but I had more than enough power. Then I got bored of that and started kicking the ball off of the sponsorship signs that circle the inner ring of the stadium. Eventually a couple security guards came to check out what the noise was all about. I stalked them for a while. I knew that I could take them both and there wouldn't be any witnesses, but I decided not to drain them because they were just a couple healthy young guys trying to make a living.

I climbed to the top of the stadium lights. I had always been afraid of heights but now that I was immortal I gave it a try. I was on my way up when my phone rang. It was my mom.

"Hey, hey," I said. "How are things in the frigid north?"

"Oh fine," She said. "It's 60 degrees and I think I'm going out with your brother and his family on the boat out this weekend. What are you up to?"

"Not too much."

"It sounds windy there."

She was right. Sort of. RFK was a bit breezy high up on the catwalk next to the lights.

"It is, a little," I said.

"How are you doing money wise? You aren't eating ramen noodles and PB and J for every meal, are you?"

Earlier in life I had been through times where I ate PB and J twice a day but not out of necessity but out of pure enjoyment. Plus living in an expensive city like DC, you learn to save every dollar.

"No, Mom," I said. "I'm not just eating PB and J."

I didn't go into telling her that I was drinking people's blood and killing them. I've always been pretty open with my mother but that was crossing a line.

"How are you really doing?" I said. "Jimmy said that you were going to the doctor, or said that you might be. You know how he is. I never know exactly what he is talking about."

"That's funny," she said. "He says the same about you. I've been feeling under the weather a bit." Then she paused. Even though I was immortal and time had ceased to have any real meaning to me, the pause felt like an eternity. "I've been tired and I've lost a bit of weight."

"When are you going to the doctor?"

"Soon. You know that I hate going to the doctor," she said. At some point most children become a parent to their own parent, if only for a moment.

"Do you want me to call and make you an appointment?"

"No. Don't be silly."

"Okay, okay."

"So what else is going on? Is Diablo still nuts?"

We talked for a little while longer, but all I could think about is that fact that my seemingly immortal mom was sick.

I jumped into my car because I needed to get out of the city to feed. It didn't seem like a great idea to only feed in DC. Even though a lot of people live there, killing a different person every week or so was a bad idea and might eventually lead the police to me.

I took the Fourth Street on ramp to I-395. There was a traffic jam, but there's always a traffic jam on the Beltway. To get across the bridge to Virginia it should've taken me twenty minutes but instead it took an hour.

The hunger started to take over so I arbitrarily got off the Falls Church exit. Once I was off the interstate I realized that the burbs at night were as busy as the city because people were still coming home from happy hours or after-work functions.

I pulled off into a random neighborhood. All of the houses looked the same. The only difference was the number on the side of the homeowners association-approved mailbox. I was wearing my jogging clothes so that I could fit in with suburbanites who claimed to be joggers but only ran on the block that they live on and then walked the rest of the time.

After a few minutes of strolling through a sort of wooded area that was crisscrossed with bike paths and residential roads, I began to cave in to my need to feed. My hands started to feel tight and my knees were getting creaky when I saw a lady with a stroller walking in front of me. I had been concentrating on stifling my hunger when she appeared from one of the other bike paths. She had a belly bump from being pregnant and her two or three year old was in a stroller made by the same company that made Hummers. There was a waddle in her walk and either her cheeks were glowing either because of her pregnancy or because she was walking for three people.

There was still time to feed without losing control, but I was getting close to the edge.

I crept up behind her and sank my fangs into her neck. At first I only felt her heartbeat but after a moment, I felt a secondary, much fainter heartbeat. When I recognized that the second beat was the baby's, I snapped out of my blood lust. The little heartbeat skipped a beat and I withdrew my fangs. Killing a mother and baby was too much. While I was drinking her blood, the mother had passed out, and I had been feeding on her while she was on the ground. I held her in my arms and her eyes were trying to flicker open.

I said, "Ma'am, are you okay?"

She looked at me confused, trying to figure out who I was and why I was holding her. "Huh? What happened?"

Then a couple from up ahead came around the corner. "Is everything all right?" The guy asked looking at me suspiciously.

"Yeah, I think," I said. " She started to pass out and I caught her."

The mother sat up and the lady came over and helped her up while the guy she was with kept looking me up and down, puffing his chest out like a rooster.

"Are you going to be all right?" I said to the mother who now had her back turned to me.

"I think so…" she said trailing off. "Can you guys walk me home?" she asked the couple.

"Yes, of course," the guy said, still looking at me like he was deciding whether or not to attack me.

She got up and started walking away with the couple. I took that as my cue to leave.

John called me and had me meet him at the spot where I had robbed his worker. When I got there he was waiting in his car and waved me over.

"I've been robbed here recently by some mortals. The problem is that I don't know if they are my mortals or if they are someone else. It started with you robbing me and now it keeps happening." He furrowed his eyebrows at me because we both knew that in a way it was my fault. I had exposed one of the weaknesses in his commerce. "I want you to follow my men and let me know how it goes. There are whispers that a competitor of mine is going to make a move on some of my employees. Don't let anyone see you. You need to be aware of your whiteness. Your lack of fear when you are in this neighborhood makes you stand out. When white people come through here they rarely take their time and they never come on foot, okay?"

"Yep," I said. "I'm a man of the shadows." I thought my line was fairly clever but it was lost on him. "Do you want me to help if they are robbed?"

"Do not save them. I don't care of they live or die. My men are expendable." John shrugged. It's easy to feel that way when the people you first learned to love had been dead for hundreds of years. "I need to know if they are trustworthy."

The opportunity seemed pretty exciting. I had only seen big drug deals on TV and I was curious about how it was going to go down. Would there be a bunch of guys with guns, Mexican stand-off style, or would two guys hand each other briefcases and it would be over with? The scariest part of a drug deal is getting killed or arrested, and I knew the odds of either one of them happening was very low given my new powers. I could feel how much stronger I had become in the past two months and as long as I kept moving, I would be almost impossible to attack.

On our way to the meeting I jogged and jumped from roof to roof. I didn't know where we were going so it was hard to keep up with the non-descript car. The car pulled around a corner and was out of my sight when the shooting started. I hadn't ever been to a war zone, but it was exactly what it I thought it would've sounded like. There was intermittent automatic gunfire from a few sources, followed by the heavy boom of a shotgun combined with glass breaking and the hollow thud of holes being punched through metal. By the time I got there the guys in the car were returning fire with the slow methodical rhythm of an experienced shooter.

The car that I had been following was riddled with bullets and the three tires I could see from behind were flat. All of the windows were blown out and smoke poured from the engine.

There were three shooters on the roofs of the buildings overlooking the car, one on my side of the street and two more on the other side. From my view I couldn't see how many people were on the ground, but I could hear yelling and see the occasional flares from guns as people returned fire on the car. The solitary light at the end of the street gave the attackers an advantage because the streetlight shone on the car but everywhere else was dark. The lack of light didn't cause me problems though.

It took me one good leap to get to the shooter on my side. I landed behind him and before he had time to turn around I picked him up and tossed him off the three-story building like a sack of trash.

Both of the shooters on the roof across the street watched him fall to his death. As I leapt to the other side, the shooter that was the farthest away from me took a shot at me but I could tell by the aim of the barrel that he wasn't going to come close. Even though he had no chance at actually hitting me, I was scared. I saw the bullet fly off to my right, spinning because of the rifling in the barrel.

Until that moment I had a God Complex about mortals. I knew that if it came down to a fight between me and them, they would lose every time. Even though I had leapt from building to building over a street the guy was still shooting at me. I was offended that he could even think about trying to shoot me. I was the apex predator in this situation and he needed to show me respect.

I landed on the other side near the guy that hadn't shot at me. He backed up, determined not to have me launch him off the roof as well. When he turned to run I jumped on him, piggy-back style. I reached around the front of his head with my right hand and got a grip on the left side of his chin. With my left hand I reached behind his head to the right side of his head with my hand near his ear and like I had seen in every Bruce Lee and Steven Seagal movie, I cranked his head in a twisting motion. His neck popped, then snapped, and then there was the sound of meat being ripped.

Meanwhile the other guy fired a shot that was low and a few feet from us. His shot was more likely to hit his buddy than me because I was still on his back. That was the second time I watched a bullet twist in the air as it came towards me. It was beautiful and if I hadn't been ripping someone's head off at the time I would have marveled at it.

I kept twisting because it was my first ninja neck break and I didn't know when to stop. The guy's body suddenly dropped away and I was left holding his head while riding his disconnected body to the ground.

The guy snapped me out of the wonderment of having yanked a head off by whistling a round past my right ear. The buzz of the bullet sounded like an insect in Jurassic Park.

Now I was offended and pissed. I yelled, "Quit shooting at me you asshole." Then I threw his friend's head at him. I missed but not by much.

I ran towards him and leapt. When I landed by him he took his last shot. It sizzled underneath my left armpit leaving a hole in my hoodie. I punched him in the middle of his chest with a deafening crunch. He dropped to his knees and then with a groan fell forward on his face. I picked him up by the back of his coat and his pants and tossed him over the side of the building. I didn't want to replicate my ninja head twist move because it was kind of gross and the last guy had bled all over me. I looked like an axe murderer.

When I looked over the side of the building. There was some shooting going on but it was slowing down, I assumed it was because guys were falling from the sky and people didn't know what was going on.

I leapt down from the top of the building and landed near the shot up car. Everyone quit shooting for a moment and watched me, wondering who the hell I was and what I was doing.

In the car, three of the four guys were dead. The living guy was seated in the back of the car and had a bullet wound in his thigh.

"Who are you?" he asked me.

"I'm here to save you," I said. Once again I felt like a superhero. "Or I can leave and let you die."

"What the hell is going on?" he asked me. He was more confused than in pain. He was in shock from being shot.

"Either you come with me now or you wait to see what they will do with you once you run out of bullets," I said. "It's up to you."

"How?"

"Let me take care of it," I said, "Just don't shoot me on accident, okay?"

He nodded yes. I saw in his eyes that no matter what he had done in the past, no matter how tough his reputation was, he was scared. So was I. A bullet zipped pass and plunked through the driver's side door and stopping on the passenger side. As if on cue, the shooting started again. I pulled him out of the car and put him on across my back, like a fireman.

We took off down the street. He yelled left and I went left. In the process of escaping my passenger took a round in the ankle, causing him to yell on impact. Beyond that, he was a soldier the whole time.

When we were a mile or so away I set him down and he made a call on his cell phone to his friend who came and picked us up.

His friend was with a young woman who got in the back of the car to take care of the wounded guy while I sat shotgun. His friend asked me who I was. I said a friend and left it at that. The driver asked us where we wanted to go and the wounded guy said, "33rd and Ames, NE."

"By RFK?" the driver asked.

"Yep," said the wounded guy, who was wincing in pain as the lady in the back poured clear alcohol on his leg. He was trying to stay cool while sucking wind through his clenched teeth.

We drove for a while and pulled in to a non-descript house on the east side of the Anacostia River. It wasn't as bad as I thought it would be. Washingtonians have it drilled into their heads that the east side of the Anacostia is a war zone but there were no bullet pocked marked houses like I would imagine. It was a typical low-income neighborhood.

We got out of the car and headed towards the house. The driver and lady stayed in the car when we got out and didn't wait until we got to the door before they drove off. I was helping the guy up the front porch when the door flew open and John was standing inside the doorway. I thought he was going to kill us both.

Outside the house was plain and the inside was just as spartan. The front room had a few couches and a TV with cable but that was it. There was nothing in the house that made it looked lived in.

John said, "You," to the wounded guy, "sit. You" he meant me, "with me." We went through a few doors. "You're lucky I don't kill you both right now and I would if you knew the fucking rules. First off, never ever, ever come to one of our homes. That gives the owner of the house the right to kill you on the spot. There is nothing more dangerous than having someone know where you live."

I immediately thought of Charlie who knew where I lived. "Secondly, what in God's name is that guy doing here? I told you not to save anyone."

"He needed help," I said. "They would have killed him."

"So what?" he said scowling at me. "Do you think that I can't replace him in a heartbeat? People are lining up to work for me in this economy."

"No." I said. "I've honestly never thought about it that way."

"And now he has been to where I live. How did you know to come here?"

"I have no idea. He gave his friend the address and we showed up. I didn't know you lived here."

The whole time he was talking he didn't move a muscle. He stood there like a statue staring holes into me while I twitched and paced with every question. I could see that he was still mulling over the option of killing us both in his head.

"Who brought you guys here?"

"I don't know. I don't know anything. I was doing what you told me to do."

"That's the problem," he said. "You didn't do what I told you to do at all. If it wasn't for his friends driving you both here, I would kill him right now, but because they drove you, I would have to kill them too or they would know where he died." He finally sat down in the only chair in the room. I wondered why there was only one chair in the room, but I wasn't in a position to ask.

"Look, man, I'm sorry. I was trying to help."

"I know but you made things worse. Now he'll think you're a superhero. Aren't there enough white superheroes in the world?"

"Yeah, good point."

"Okay. Lets go out and talk to him. No, I'll talk, you listen."

John walked out into the room and the wounded guy was sitting on the floor next to the couch.

"Hey X, I didn't want to get any blood on your couch. Sorry I got a little on your floor." His bleeding had stopped but the bandages were pretty miserable looking and would need to be changed soon.

"It will be fine. Here is the deal for both of you. Neither of you have ever been here. If anyone asks you about tonight, tell them that you were dropped off at the wrong house. I don't care where. Do you understand?" he didn't wait for us to tell him that we understood because it was pretty straightforward. "Here is some cash for the hospital." He said to the other guy and tossed him a wad of money held together by a rubber band. "You are excused." The guy got up and hobbled to the door. John helped him out by opening it and once he was out he shut the door.

"As for you, this should help your money issues." He gave me a roll of hundreds that was bigger than I had ever seen in my life. "I appreciate you saving my guy but next time I pay you to do something, follow my directions. I don't like to do this but I can't have you coming around my house. You clearly don't belong here and I don't want to raise any suspicions with the neighbors. If I see you on the east side of the Anacostia River, besides just passing through, I'm going to have to kill you. I won't want to but I will. I can't afford to jeopardize all I've done to create a solid life here. That is the way it is. No hard feelings."

"Okay." I said. And then I left. I resented the fact that he had threatened my life but I understood. I wasn't used to being talked to that way. That was the first time anyone had every told me that they would kill me and had the means and guts to do it. I started walking home, after all, I was only a few miles from my house. When I was on the Whitney Young Memorial Bridge heading towards RFK stadium it started to drizzle rain. By the time I was all the way across it was pouring on me. I considered running home but there wasn't a point. I was as wet as I could possibly be.

CHAPTER 12

I snuck in through the back window of the hospice. Most of the windows were open because it was warm out with a gentle breeze. I crept down the hallway and passed a partially open door when I heard someone say, "James, there you are. You came back for me. I knew you would. They said you wouldn't but I knew you would." Her voice was barely above a whisper.

I stopped. I didn't think that I was her James but the way she said "I knew you would" made me look in through her door. I didn't want to let her down if she thought I was her James. There was no one else in the hallway.

"Oh James. It has been so long," she said. "How have you been?"

I went inside the room and stood at the foot of her bed. I didn't want to get caught, so I listened to see if anyone was coming down the hallway at the sound of her voice but no one noticed. I had hoped that I could take someone while they slept because the last time I had a conversation with my dinner I left hungry.

"I've been good," I said. "How are you?"

She was so little and skinny that it was hard to tell the difference between the rumpled blankets and her limbs. Her hair had big gray curls and was spread out all over her pillow as if she had a head of dandelion fluff.

"You know how I have been James," she said. "You have been with me the whole time."

"Yes, I have," I said. I smiled as sincerely as I could. When people are that sick, looking at them feels intrusive, like watching a private moment that no one else should be a part of. I wanted to look away from her, to give her privacy but that would've been rude.

Her soft green cataract filled eyes started to glisten wet.

"Please have a seat. Or is it time to go?"

She started to move around like she was going to get up. Even though she didn't weigh much I doubted that her little bones would be able to handle it.

"No, no. I came for a visit."

"So it isn't time for me yet? I'm so tired. Please. I can't do this anymore." Her bottom lip started to tremble and a few tears rolled slowly down her cheeks until they ran out of energy and stopped along her jaw line.

"I'm here for to visit, okay? Maybe it will be time to go soon," I said.

I didn't know what to do. She clearly wanted to leave and the only way she was in a body bag. Her room had no personal effects or any indication that anyone had ever come to see her.

"Will you please take me with you," she said. "I would like to go now." She tried to raise her voice but she didn't have the strength.

I stood next to her bed facing her. I put my hand on top of hers. She tried to look at me and smile but her eyes were so bad that she was looking somewhere off to my left.

I leaned down. As gently as possible, I pierced the carotid artery in her neck. She flinched only for a second and then leaned into my teeth. After two spurts of blood the rest dribbled out into my mouth. Then she was gone. She was so close to death that all she had needed was a little nudge. I left and for the first time since I had turned I didn't feel guilty about killing someone. I was able to convince myself that she was going to die that night, whether I had visited her or not.

My phone rang less than a minute after the sun went down. Without looking at it I knew it was either Andrew or another vampire. The timing was too good. I climbed out from in between my mattress and box spring. I couldn't buy a coffin and drag it downstairs into my place to sleep in. There are too many people who live on my block who might see me with it. Besides, thought of sleeping in coffin was too creepy to me and I drink blood.

The number said private. I hoped it wasn't a bill collector because even though I had a fair amount of money, I couldn't put it in my bank because I didn't have a job and if anyone investigated me it would look suspicious. Paying bills seemed like such a normal, mortal thing to do and I wasn't a normal mortal any more.

"Hello," I said.

"Stephen, this is John. I need to speak with you. Meet me at Stanton Park in a half an hour." Then he hung up.

I got up, put some clothes on, leashed up Diablo and left the house. Summer was in full swing and even though it was dark out, the air was so thick with humidity that it would have been easier to swim than to walk.

When we got there John was sitting on a park bench that was facing the direction we arrived from. With his vision he was able to see pretty far down Massachusetts Avenue. If he didn't know where I lived before that meeting, he had narrowed it down to a pretty small area. He sat there until we got to him, not bothering to get up. I sat down on the far side from him leaving the middle of the bench open. As usual he was wearing a suit, dark blue with pinstripes and a light gray tie.

Diablo was at the full extent of her leash staying as far from John as she could get. Even though I'm bigger than John, he is far more intimidating. His cold eyes and an expressionless face were a poker player's dream. It worked wonders in his line of work.

"Your dog appears to have an aversion to me," he said.

"You're kind of a scary guy," I said.

"So I have been told. I guess a walking nightmare in a ten thousand dollar suit is still a nightmare," he said.

"I think of myself more as a monster than a nightmare."

"A monster? Perhaps you are. I am sure that Leanne Washington's parents would agree with you. When I think of monsters, I think of Frankenstein with screws in his neck and a lot of single octave moaning. On the other hand, nightmares inspire absolute fear. Nightmares have existed since the dawn of time and so have we. Monsters tend to drool and get slain by torch bearing villagers. I encourage you to avoid both."

"Nightmares aren't real though." Even though I meant it, at the same time I was questioning myself because until a few months ago I didn't think that vampires existed either.

"It is better if the villagers think that we are not real either."

"Fair enough. Have they ever found out that we are real?" This was a concern of mine because the pastor at the church obviously knew.

"From time to time. It never ends well for the mortals. The story of us is a perfect example of how fact becomes legend and then myth. There are stories of vampires that date back to the 13th century and some even before that in India. At some point everything that scares people becomes just another story to tell by the campfire. If one was to multiply a single story by a hundred it becomes myth. Basically it is a version of the children's game called Telephone. Where one child says one thing to the next until the end and the message had changed. Generation after generation beating a story into fantasy because each version is more interesting and improved until the original is lost."

We both looked around for a minute and watched the fresh-faced interns and the new college grads stumbling home from the bar after too many happy hour drinks. We were two eagles watching the unaware salmon swim upstream.

"I suppose I should be getting to the point of our meeting. The attack on my men was an attack on me personally. We both know that you showed everyone in my business that there are flaws in my security, and even though no mortal could have done what you were able to do, it made my rivals think I was someone who could be attacked. In my line of business I cannot afford to show weakness whether it is real or perceived. Given your money woes, I have an offer."

I nodded.

"I want revenge but I need it to be done in a discreet manner. If I wanted to have a huge show of force I could pay a couple teams of hit men to go over there and turn their neighborhood into a battle field but then it would turn into an all out war and I don't want to resort to that yet. It would be too costly and I would like to send a subtle message. Still interested?"

"Of course. Those guys at shot me too."

"I forgot about that. You don't seem to have any lasting effects." Then he smiled.

I grinned. Vamp humor isn't all that great but it was nice to have an inside joke.

"Okay. Be on the southwest corner of 8th and East Capitol Street tomorrow before midnight and I will send someone for you. He will tell you about our rivals and take you close to where they operate. You will have to find your own way home because I can't have anyone be seen with you. As you may have heard the other night my men call me X and I expect you to do the same in their presence. How does $10,000 sound?"

"That works for me."

He handed me an envelope that was solid and thick but the size didn't come close to conveying how much money was in the envelope or what I was going to do to earn it.

"Do you want me to call you when it is over?" I asked.

"No. I'll contact you when the time is right."

I didn't have any idea about how I would contact him if I wanted to, short of going and robbing his employees again.

The next night I was at the designated corner at midnight when a beat up old red Ford Taurus pulled up to the corner and stopped. The young black male driving the car waved me in. When I got in the car it smelled like old fast food and cheap cigars.

"You're the guy who robbed Troy?" He said. I was a little offended his dismissive tone.

"I have no idea what you are talking about," I said.

"Yeah right. People on the block are wondering why you aren't dead yet."

"Yeah, me too. Tell me about where we are going and what my plan should be."

I figured John wouldn't want me talking to his employees any more than I had to.

I got out of the car with a little information about how their operation worked. I was out of my element, north of the Hill and near the dividing line between northeast and northwest.

The setup was simple, more or less like John's, but because this other group had a higher volume of traffic and moved more product, they had more people and better security.

I put a ten-dollar bill in my coat pocket for easy access because the driver told me that the easiest way for me to the see the operation was to try to buy some drugs myself.

From down the block I watched a few transactions, then slowly walked up the street. Aside from the small area where they were selling drugs, I could have been anywhere in the city.

I walked up to the first guy and said, "Ten."

In retrospect I realize that I'm an idiot. I clearly had no idea what I was doing.

My hand was on my money and was starting to pull it out when he said, "Ten what? What are you talking about? You a cop?"

"Do I look like a cop to you?" I said.

I could feel my fangs start to creep down, as he looked me up and down trying to figure out if I was actually a cop. My instinct was to kill this clown and move on but he was the absolute bottom of their supply chain and I was looking for someone a little more substantial.

"What do you want?"

"I need a fix." I didn't even know what a fix was but it sounded desperate enough.

He put out his hand and took the money. Then he made a hand signal to the guys at the end of the block. They stopped talking and turned to face me. For the first time since the gun fight, mortals were making me anxious. I wasn't nervous about getting beat up or hurt because even though there were three of them, I knew without a shadow of a doubt that I could destroy them if I wanted to. My nerves were remnants from when I was a boy and I got picked on in a schoolyard. These guys looked down on me like these three guys at my elementary school. My older brother would protect me when he was around, but when he wasn't there was a group of three boys who would call me a queer and make fun of me for answering questions in class.

I started walking towards them and they headed right towards me. The streetlight made their faces hard to see because only one out of every four or five lights worked. What I could see though was startling.

The guy on the far left had a sneer on his face like my childhood nemesis Clay had. His sneer meant trouble. All of the times when I had my backpack taken off my back and thrown into the drainage ditch, every moment of having my face mashed into the gritty snow, when I felt like I was suffocating.

My fangs came out.

When the dealers were twenty feet from me, the demons that had been hidden in the past surged back. I knew now that everything had changed and there was nothing I could do to change it back. I was going to live forever and these chumps didn't stand a chance. No one would ever pick on me again.

With a blur I flew at the guy with the sneer and pushed him as hard as I could. His feet left the ground and for a moment he was parallel to the ground. He made a weak attempt to grab on to my sleeves to catch himself as his arms came up but he missed. He bounced off of the side of a parked car and landed on the sidewalk in a heap.

The guy in the middle turned to react to me, I swung my open palm and hit him in the adam's apple so hard that something popped. He fell to his knees with both hands on his throat, making a gurgling sound.

I turned on the last guy when the red and blue lights started flashing. There were two undercover cop cars converging on us from both sides of the street.

The last guy ran for it. I didn't know if he was running from the police or me. Neither option was going to turn out well from him.

The first guy had pulled a gun while he was on the ground. I walked over to him at regular human speed. At that moment, I was sure that he couldn't kill me with it and I wasn't afraid. He fired and the bullet hit me in the left shoulder. The bullet burned my skin as it passed through, and while he may not be able to kill me, it still really hurt. I know how ridiculous it sounds now but with my newly developed God complex, I didn't think that anything could hurt me.

The bullet knocked me off balance throwing my left side back. He shot again and the bullet buzzed past my left ear. I went over to him, reached down and grabbed his left ankle with my right hand. Then I pivoted my hips and swung him like you would swing a bat with one hand. We were close to a streetlight so when I swung him at the post he connected fully with his head. The sound was like dropping a watermelon off of a roof onto a metal table.

Before I could turn around there were two spotlights aimed at my back.

"Put your hands on your head," said an authoritative voice over the loudspeaker.

I started to put my hands up slowly. I heard four car doors open behind me. My left shoulder hurt as I began to raise it but I could feel it mending slowly. It had that itchy feeling of skin trying to fix itself.

Looking at the wall, I had two shadows, one from each light. The light from each of the spotlights caused the other shadow to be a little lighter. I thought, now there are three of us, with our hands up but none of us are going to be put in cuffs.

"Down on your knees. Now!" said the voice.

I started to bend my knees for a moment like I was getting down. Then I turned to my left and ran, keeping my face turned away from them so that they couldn't identify me. I was gone in an instant. They didn't have a chance to chase me.

CHAPTER 14

I was wandering around H Street half-heartedly looking for a victim because I wanted to get my hands on fresh, younger blood instead of strays or people who were knocking on death's door. Whenever I thought about killing someone young, the news stories with Leanne's mom crying on TV about their murdered daughter popped into my head.

I had found someone to stalk when my cell phone vibrated and scared the shit out of me. The number came up as private, which made me uneasy. Who was calling me and what did they have to hide? I was tired of private calls so I decided not to answer and sent the call straight to voicemail.

As I was trying to regain my composure, my former coworker Megan came out of a group she was standing in and gave me a running hug.

"Hey," I said.

"Hey you." she said. "How's life and such?" She was drunk and her words were all pouring out at the same time with no pauses between them. "I'm out with these people over here." She pointed at the group she was with and teeter-tottered from her heels to the balls of her feet and then back again.

My ringtone indicated that there was a voicemail on my phone.

"Life's been good," I said, not wanting to pursue it. I couldn't tell her anything. "Have you been crying every day now that I quit?" I was trying to lighten the moment and turn the conversation back to her.

"Oh my gosh, you quit?" she said with a smile. "I didn't even notice." Then she looked into my eyes for a moment. "You're cute. Boop." Her boop coincided with using her forefinger to tap the end of my nose.

"Wow. You've had enough to drink to think I'm cute? It's probably time to call it a night."

"I have to go back to my friends but you should call me some time, okay?"

"I will." I said, knowing that I wouldn't. "Have a good night."

"I'm serious. Call me."

"Okay, okay."

She gave me a hug that lasted a little longer than the traditional hug but I didn't mind.

Then a text message came in from Charlie. It had been a while since I had heard from her so I was hoping that she was looking for a booty call. She wasn't. She had sent me one of those pictures where someone holds the camera at the end of their fully extended arm so they can take a picture of themselves and someone or something else. The someone else was Andrew, asleep in his bed. At first glance I thought he was dead but it was my eyes playing tricks on me. There was too much blood in his cheeks.

I called Charlie. It didn't even ring on my end before she picked up.

"What the fuck are you doing?" I was pissed but I made sure to keep control of my tongue because no matter how mad I was, I knew that she would have no problems killing him and then me.

"I thought that would get your attention, love," she said. I could hear her smile on the other end of the phone.

"Yes. You have it. Get out of my house."

"Oh I don't have to." she said, "You invited me in all those months ago and now you can't uninvite me because you are one of us."

"So talk. What do you want from me?" I said.

I was getting nervous that Andrew would wake up and freak the out. If he did I couldn't blame him. There was also the off chance that Charlie would decide to kill him for some reason that I wasn't aware of yet.

"I wanted your attention, Love. That's all." she said again with another whisper.

"I know you said that already." I wanted to yell but I thought that Andrew might wake up if I raised my voice.

"Good. I'm glad that you understand." Then she hung up. I tried to call her back but I went straight to voicemail.

I started pacing back and forth, I didn't know what to do. My best friend was in danger because of someone that I had brought home. I called Andrew.

"Yeah?" He mumbled.

"Oh sorry," I said. "I butt-dialed you." I knew that it didn't make sense because if I called him on accident from my pocket I wouldn't know that he was on the phone. I hoped his sleepiness would it slide.

Then I hung up.

A short time later my phone rang. I groped in my pocket hoping that it was Charlie calling me back, but it was my mom.

"Hi Mom."

"Hi Tubby. Whatcha up to?"

"Not much. Getting ready take Diablo out to wander for a bit. How about you?"

"Isn't it a little late to take the dog out for a walk?"

"Um, yeah. It won't be a very long walk. I need to make sure that she doesn't have to pee in the middle of the night and wake me up."

I thought to myself, "nice move, idiot." I was trying to stay under the radar but I couldn't even keep my mouth shut about going out for a nighttime stroll in one of the most dangerous cities in the country. I knew that when I went on a stroll that I wouldn't have anything to worry about, but she didn't.

"I went to the doctor today. I hate how long they make you wait, even if you have an appointment."

"Yeah, me too." I wanted to tell her that I was shot and I didn't even have to go to the doctor because I had healed myself but that would have led to more questions. "How did it go?"

"Well," she paused. I had my fan on for Diablo because it was hot outside and during her pause I was looking at it. Time slowed down. I could see each individual fin on the fan. "They have to do a biopsy on a few of my lymph nodes."

"They think you have cancer?" Even though it is against the rules to change a member of your family (punishable by death), I immediately wanted to turn her into one of us so that she would live forever.

"The doctor doesn't know so they are going to check."

I wanted to ask her if I could borrow some money to fly home but there weren't flights that only went between sunset and sunrise.

"Should I come home?" I asked.

"Oh no. Don't be ridiculous. It is a simple procedure and it will probably turn out to be nothing."

The key word repeated itself in my head. Probably, probably, probably, probably.

"Are you sure?"

"Yes. There is no reason to talk about it any more," she said with enough force to remain nice but to let me know that this part of the conversation was over.

We talked for a little while longer but I don't remember what was said. The words biopsy and her voice saying, "will probably turn out to be nothing, probably, probably" drowned out everything else.

With nothing else to do I went up to the National Cathedral. I hadn't started believing in God all of a sudden but if there was a deity upstairs I figured that the cathedral would be the place to get in touch with it. If anything, I thought I might be able to get my mom some credit into heaven even if I didn't stand a chance getting in.

The cathedral was even larger that I had imagined. It was at least twenty stories high and built out of big, grey blocks that would have made St. Peter proud. At first glance I thought my eyes were playing tricks on me because on the northeast corner one of the gargoyles was Darth Vader's head, but there he was in all of his galactic splendor. I went over to the huge front doors of the church and looked way up to the steeple at the top. Even with my strength, I was pretty sure that I wouldn't be able to jump to the first roof level that was more than ten stories up. I wanted to try so that I could pose like a superhero in a movie, but there was too much light on the building. I didn't need the extra attention anyway.

One of the sisters from the abbey approached me. She looked to be in her mid-30s. Her light green eyes and well-defined cheekbones stood in sharp contrast to the black and white blandness of her habit.

"Do you think you could jump up there?" she asked me. I was still looking up but when she asked me that I turned my focus on her. My look caused her to flinched a little.

"I was thinking about it, and probably not," I answered honestly. I was a little surprised that she knew what I was, but if the pastor knew how to kick me out of his church then a long-standing religion like Catholicism probably had my kind dialed in pretty well. I assumed that she knew more about my people than I did.

"No?" she said with a little surprise. "You must be fairly new then." Then she smiled at me. "Would you like to come in?"

"Sure." I wondered if she had some trick up her sleeve. I was concerned that something awful was going to happen to me when I entered the church, but if you can't trust a nun then who can you trust.

"Wait here please." She went inside and came out with another nun who was in her 60s or 70s.

"Hello," said the older woman. She had a stern voice and looked like a mean grandma. "You aren't here for mischief are you?"

"No ma'am." To this day I don't know why I called her ma'am. That was the first time I had ever called anyone ma'am.

She turned and led me inside with the younger nun walking behind me. If the church was designed to put the parishioners in awe of its size and therefore in awe of God, it worked on me. The front part of the church was at least as big as a football field and filled with rows and rows of dark stained wooden chairs. There were large flat screen TVs spaced from front to back so that no matter where you were you would be able to see the ceremony. On both sides of the entrance running the length of the church were big marble columns and stained glass. It disappointed me that I wouldn't ever be able to see the sunlight shine through them.

I sat in the back row, flanked on both sides by my escorts.

"So what brings you to our church?" the elder nun asked.

"The same thing as everyone else, I guess, a crisis of faith." I was surprised by my honesty for the second time.

"I didn't know that people with your condition had faith as us mortals understand it," said the younger nun earning herself a glare from the older nun.

"I'm still trying to figure it all out," I said. "I'm pretty new at this." Towards the front of the church there were some confessionals. Without thinking about my actions I focused on them and I heard someone say, "Forgive me father, for I have sinned. It has been six weeks since my last confession..." Then I felt a hand softly land on my hand. It was the older sister.

"Please respect the privacy of the people in the confessionals." She said it sternly enough to let me know that she was serious while maintaining her grace.

"Sorry, I didn't mean to. I didn't..." then my voice trailed off. The first part of the sentence was a lie and I didn't see the need to keep going with it. "I'm here because my mom is going to die and there isn't anything I can do about it. I'm immortal, she isn't."

The elder nun put her hand on the back of the chair in front of her and helped herself up. "Let's walk a little." She said already starting to walk towards the far wall.

I got up because I didn't have a choice in the matter. The elder nun waited at the end of the pew and walked next to me while the younger one walked behind us.

"You must be very young for your people if your mother is alive," She said looking at me out of the corner of her eye.

I nodded. She kept walking and then looked at me again.

"I'm here because everyone is going to die before me." I said it louder than I had intended to.

"Yes, that must be a great burden for you to bear." For a moment, I felt like she understood me. In a lot of ways, both of us were destined to lead solitary lives.

"Yeah, it is. But there is nothing I can do about it."

"It sounds like you have part of your answer right there." We walked for a little while longer and she led me to the front of the church and out the doors. "I regret having to say this, but you aren't invited into the church any more. If you would like to return, we will let you in again, we can't let you come and go as you please. I hope you understand."

"I do and thank you."

She smiled and nodded.

CHAPTER 15

I was sitting on my couch watching TV with the dog when my phone rang. I was tired of my phone ringing. Either it was bad news from my mom or people making me do shit. For someone who didn't have a job and drank people's blood I was more popular than I should have been.

I pressed talk and before I could say hello, I heard, "This is Simon. Please meet me at Café Park by Lincoln Park in 10 minutes." Then he hung up. I remember thinking to myself that vampires never ask me if I want to meet them or at least how I'm doing. I put my clothes on as fast as I could. I was annoyed but wasn't going to make Simon wait. I put on pair of shorts and a polo shirt with some sneakers, because flip-flops weren't cut out for vampire fun.

The moon was so big that night that I howled at it under my breath. I was half a block from the restaurant when a black Lincoln Town Car rolled down its window. Simon looked out and told me to get in. I got in the back and all of a sudden I felt under dressed. Simon was dressed in a suit and so was the driver, a middle-aged looking white guy. Freaking vamps dressed up for everything.

"Good morning," he said, even though it was about an hour after sunset. "This is Roger." He nodded at the driver. "We have a few things to discuss with you."

The automatic doors locked and Roger looked at me in the rearview mirror. I didn't doubt for a moment that I could be out the window and down the street in less than a second or two at the most, but I was also sure that both of them were much faster than I was so escaping would be impossible. I stayed put.

The windows were so tinted that it was hard for me to see out them even with my vamptastic eyesight.

"Where are we going?" I said.

"There are some people that would like to talk to you. Don't worry, you aren't in any sort of trouble."

"Okay," I sighed. I didn't bother asking any more questions because the sound of his voice told me that I wasn't going to get anywhere. I understood the need for secrecy against mortals but I was one of them. They still didn't consider me as an equal.

We drove northwest, between Union Station and the capitol. Even though Simon told me that I wasn't in trouble, I wondered if it would be the last time that I would see either of them. We stopped in Chinatown and parked in an alley. Simon got out. When I pulled the handle to get out the door was locked by the child safety feature.

"We're staying," Roger told me flatly.

"Yeah, I guess we are," I said.

Then I saw Charlie come out of one of the doors down the side street. She saw Simon coming for her and turned to run. He was too fast for her and slammed her against the ground. While she was recovering he pulled on the head of his cane and a silver chain came out of it. He held on to the top of the cane and the bottom wooden part of the cane while he hogtied her hands and feet with the chain. She tried to squirm, but each time the chain would cut her skin she would moan in pain. Her fangs were out and she was snapping at Simon but he didn't care. Simon reached into his pocket and put on a set of leather gloves. He picked up Charlie by the chain and started walking to the car. I was sitting near the side he was approaching and I scooted over but it was for nothing. Roger popped the trunk and Simon unceremoniously dropped her in and shut it. Simon got back in the car.

"I wish it didn't come to this," he said to no one in particular.

We pulled out and headed northwest on Massachusetts Avenue. A few minutes into the drive, Simon handed me a soft bag that was covered in black silk on the inside and outside.

"Please put the bag on your head," he said. "I know it is a little undignified but it is necessary."

I tried to pay attention to where were going from under the depths of my hood by counting the lefts and the rights but after a few of each I lost track and gave up.

They pulled me out of the car and Roger (I think) guided me down a long chilly hallway. I wasn't around when they pulled Charlie out of the trunk but it would have been fun to watch. At the beginning of the ride she yelled at us to let her out but after a few minutes she stopped.

When they took the bag off of my head I was in a big circular room with marble columns around the wall. The ceiling was at least 40 feet high and it was painted like St. Peter's Basilica in Rome if Michelangelo had been using drugs and reading too much Bram Stoker. Part of the painting was a mural of the capitol at night with vampires sitting on the roof and lurking in the background. Carved into the floor in a circle that was smaller circle that said, "In Dubio Pro Reo". Inside the circle was a map of DC, Virginia, and Maryland. I couldn't remember my Latin from college very well but I think the saying on the floor meant "In Doubt For" the something. I didn't know the last word.

The room was bright and reflective because of the shine off of the white marble. The marble was the same color as the bottom ring of the Washington Monument. It took me a minute to get my bearings because it was the first time I had been in a room so bright since I had turned.

When I was able to focus, I saw three vampires sitting at a marble judge's bench. They looked at me with some curiosity. Simon pointed me to a single chair that had a table in front of it and told me to sit down so I sat. The room was dead quiet.

"What is your name?" said a lady in an all black robe with her hood up. She had black hair and blue eyes and was strikingly beautiful in the same way that a peacock is with all of its feathers up. She was sitting in the middle with a man to her left and another female to her right. All of them were wearing black robes but she was the only one with the hood up.

"Steve. Um, Stephen. Brooks. Stephen Brooks," I said. I wanted to mock myself and tell them that my mom drank a lot when she was pregnant but they didn't seem like the jokey types. Add to the fact that I was scared shitless and, well, witless.

"Are you sure?"

"Yes, ma'am. I'm sure."

"Do you know why you are here?"

"No ma'am. Simon didn't say anything about where I was going or why."

"Did you ask?"

"I don't remember. I don't think so. I figured that I would find out soon enough."

"You are here because we want to talk to you about Chantal-Genevieve Leglise. I think you know her as Charlie."

I nodded.

"Yes, ma'am," I said a little too loudly. "Okay." I hated showing how nervous they made me but I couldn't control myself.

"Please bring her out." And there was Charlie. A man in a black robe pushed her out to face the judges on a rolling cart. She was hanging by the silver handcuffs on her wrist and ankles. There was a chain connected to the bar above her head that looped down to a silver collar around her neck. She was in shorts and a tee shirt and wasn't moving at all. She had been gorgeous before and now she looked disheveled and wild. There were burn marks around the places where the silver had been touching her.

"Did you know her before she turned you?"

"No. I mean I knew her for a few hours I guess. I don't really remember meeting her or anything. I was pretty drunk."

"Please tell us what you can remember."

So I did, with as much detail as I could remember. They didn't stop me for clarification or ask me any questions. I had a hard time concentrating because that was the first time that I had three sets of vampire eyes staring at me at the same time. The intensity of them looking at me was a physical weight that I felt on my forehead and in my eyes. At one point I had to shut my eyes so that I could concentrate. I'm glad that I didn't have anything to lie about because I have no doubt that they would have known. Not because they have super mind reading power but because they read every facial twitch and heard my heartbeat. The three of them had been around long enough to know when someone was lying. They didn't twitch a muscle the whole time. When I was finished speaking, the two people flanking the main judge handed her pieces of paper. They looked at each other for a few moments, communicating with their eyes.

"Tell us about Leanne Washington."

"It was my first time feeding," I said. "I'm sorry if I caused trouble. I kept drinking as she was dying and I think that is why I got sick but maybe not. I don't know why. I honestly don't remember much about what happened. My body took over. I've learned to be more discreet now."

"How have you been exercising your new-found discretion?"

"I've been going to this hospice every once in a while to feed on some people who are dying because I figured that if they are dying, no one will notice when they die because that is what they are supposed to do."

The other lady judge smiled a little bit with one side of her mouth and then caught herself and stopped.

"Did you ask Charlie to change you?" The judge burrowed down even deeper with her stare when she asked me.

"No. I woke up and I was changed."

"Did you meet anyone else that she had changed?"

"Yeah, some guy but I don't remember his name."

"Thank you," she said. "That is all." I got up and Simon directed me to a solitary chair on the side of the room.

Then she said, "Please put forward the accused."

For the first time I was able to get a good look at Charlie without the distracting questions. Charlie was rolled out, chained and inside of a silver cage that glistened in the bright lights of the room. She looked fearless. Our eyes met for only a moment and then I looked away.

"Do you wish to be called Charlie or Chantal?" The head judge asked her.

"Charlie is fine," she said. "We both know that it isn't going to matter soon."

"Okay," said the judge and then she sighed. "Let's proceed then. We warned you several times that it is illegal by our district code to create another without our consent but you continued to do it anyway. What do you have to say for yourself?"

"Nothing really," Charlie responded. She sounded small inside the cage. I wanted to free her and promise them that she wouldn't ever do it again. "I was bored. Living forever with the same people isn't living at all. Once you have heard someone's opinions and personal history over the past 100 years, they don't matter any more. The mortals I created were more fun to talk to than all of you combined. I wanted to add someone new to my life. I like meeting people who can give me another perspective that I haven't thought of before. Why would I want to keep my life static? This life we live is boring. It is no wonder that old people don't mind dying. After a while it is time to call it the end. I'm sick of this life."

"Is that why you continued to make others? So that you could have fun with them, hunt and then kill them?"

"No. Some of them were too big of risks. They were killing people on sidewalks or they would go insane so I had to put them down like a rabid dog. I have to admit, putting them down was fun. Hunting humans is so easy but hunting vampires, even new ones, gave me a thrill."

"And lastly, how do you respond to the accusation that you gave mortals information about Stephen's domicile?"

I sat up straight. I had wondered how those guys had found out where I lived.

"Yeah," Charlie said, "That was me." For the first time, she actually looked like she felt bad about her actions. She looked at me and then looked away.

"No one poses a bigger risk to our way of life than you do, and for that you must be punished." The judge slid a piece of paper to the other woman judge and then to the male who then handed it back to her. She looked down at the paper. "By vinculum juris, when the sun rises tomorrow morning, you shall be there to greet it." Then the judges got up and left through a door to the right of room.

The guy, who had wheeled Charlie out, came back out and took her away. She didn't even flinch. I wanted to tell her that I forgave her and that I knew what it was like to be lonely but I don't think it would've mattered.

I started to get up and Simon told me to stay seated. Then he told me that I was made illegally and that the judges had left the room to decide my fate. I felt sick to my stomach.

They came back a few minutes later and told me that I was allowed to remain in the district as long as I abided by their rules. I was given one chance. Then they left the room.

I got back in the car with Roger and Simon. I wanted to ask about Charlie's fate but I knew that once I learned, I wouldn't be able to unlearn it, so I kept my mouth shut.

I was coming home from getting Diablo some dog food when I saw one of the guys from when we were ambushed. Well, I wasn't ambushed, and John's men were but semantics were beside the point. He was two blocks from my house and taking his sweet time looking around. Either he was trying to be sneaky and doing a horrible job or he was sending a message to me on behalf of his boss to let me know they were looking for me. He wasn't dressed as some gangster thug from the projects; he was in jeans and a Washington Nationals tee shirt. He didn't look different than anyone else in the neighborhood.

He was looking around at the houses for an address that he couldn't find. If I hadn't seen his face so clearly before he turned and ran off that night, I might not have thought anything about him being on my block.

My first instinct was to kill him but I was tired of killing people so I settled on watching him for the time being.

I knew that I couldn't have these guys coming to look for me at Andrew's house. Andrew and Anne had nothing to do with it and I was bringing danger to their doorstep. I leapt to the roof of a condo building that was a block away from where he was so that I would be able to see him without him knowing. He lingered around for a bit and started walking up my block. When he got to my house he walked through our short yard and knocked on the door. I started to move closer but if he pulled a gun out and started shooting at whomever answered the door, I wouldn't be able to save them.

Then my fangs came out. I didn't know if it meant that there was another vampire around or if it was due to my nerves.

Anne came to the door but didn't open it. They had two doors to get to the outside and she didn't open either of them.

"Can I help you?" Anne shouted through the double doors. She was looked out the long, thin window that was next to the door.

"I think that I have the wrong house," he said. "Sorry." Then he turned around and walked off.

Anne watched him go, peeking through the curtains from the living room.

They knew where I lived. The game was up. I leapt off of the roof and followed him. He was heading north towards Kingman Park. He wasn't aware that I was following him but I was paranoid that he was leading me into a trap.

I was livid at my own stupidity. Charlie had led them right to me and now I was putting my friends in danger. Just because I had been through a change didn't mean that I had to screw up everyone else's lives.

The time for following him was over. I had to do something. I snuck up behind him and grabbed him by the back of his neck. Over the last few months I was much stronger than I had ever been so my hand was like a vise grip. I was squeezing hard enough to make his head look up a little bit. He was trying to look tough while his hand was moving slowly down towards whatever he had in his pockets so I punched him in the stomach. He doubled over and threw up, almost getting puke on my shoes.

I picked him back up so that we could keep walking. While he was wiping his mouth I went through his pockets, and pulled out his .22 caliber Saturday Night Special that he was carrying even though it was a Wednesday. I tossed it into the bushes. I found his wallet and Metro Card and took them.

As I held him by his neck we started walking down the street. To a casual onlooker, it wouldn't have looked like I was hurting him at all.

"I know who sent you and why so I'm going to make this short," I said.

I pulled out his driver's license and looked at his name and address.

"Cecil Robinson of 1721 43rd Street Southeast, the next time I see you," I said, "I'm going to kill everyone who lives at this address."

And then I stomped my foot down as hard as I could on top of his foot. I heard it break. He cried out in pain and his legs went weak but I continued to hold him up by the back of his neck.

"And I'm going to kill everyone you have ever met if I ever see you again." Even as I said it I knew it was an empty threat because I wasn't going to murder his second grade teacher but I wanted to get my point across.

Then I turned and kneed him in the balls. He doubled over so hard that I had to let him fall to the ground.

"If you think this is bad," I said, "Wait until you find out what I'm going to do to you next time."

He was on the ground doubled over, trying to hold his nuts and his foot at the same time. I kicked him in the face, not very hard, and his blood spattered everywhere. I pulled my kick because I knew that if I didn't, I could kick him hard enough to kill him. He wasn't quite unconscious but he was woozy, and trying to say something. His phone vibrated. I answered it.

"Come get Cecil. He's south of Kingman Park on 17th," I said. Then I hung up.

CHAPTER 16

I was sitting at home watching The Wonder Years when my brother called. We didn't talk that much. It isn't that we had a problem with each other but we didn't need to talk. We were different people.

"Hey James," I said. "What's up?"

"Hey Tubby," Jimmy said. "You need to come home. Soon."

"I'm great," I said. "Thanks for asking."

It didn't take long to remember why I only talked to him a few times a year, over e-mail.

"Don't be a whiny bitch," he said. "I'm being serious. Mom is sick and it's time for you to come home."

"I know she is sick." Then I thought about it. "How sick is she?"

"Like months to live sick." His usually confident voice began to waver a bit.

"Jesus. Okay. I need a little time to conjure up some money."

"Take out some credit cards and max them out," he said. "I don't give a shit. Get up here. Don't plan on coming home for a week or something. We need you here until…"

"I know," I said. "I'll make it happen."

After he told me what to do the tone turned a little more conversational. Eventually he asked me how I was doing.

I needed money to get home and to pay rent because even though I didn't have a lease or a signed document I wanted to pay for an additional month to Andrew because I was leaving on short notice.

Robbing a jewelry store was the only answer that I could come up with. I had thought about doing it before but I didn't because it was a dangerous proposition. Desperate times call for desperate measures. There would be lots of cameras and witnesses so I would have to be smart about it. I wasn't quite sure how I would sell the jewelry that I was going to steal but I figured that John might be able to help me find a way.

My plan was to walk over to Georgetown and find a jewelry store that would be open late enough after the sunset for me to get there. When the time was right I would pull a face mask on, run in and rob the place. I couldn't use the Metro there or back because of the cameras so I would have to walk.

Walking back I would go through the residential areas because they provide for more options for cover than walking on the Mall or through downtown with the all office buildings that had security in the street level lobbies.

There was a jewelry store on Wisconsin Avenue that was open until 8:00 and the sun sets in September around 7:00, so I had to move pretty quickly to make it up there in time. I wanted to wait around for a few more months because then I would have more time, but I needed to get to Alaska as soon as possible.

I put on a jogging outfit and trekked to Georgetown. I ran pretty fast but not fast enough to cause people to notice me.

As I got closer, I checked my watch and it said 7:37. I put my hand in my pocket to make sure that my red bandanna was still in there. Originally I wanted to get a Ronald Reagan or Hillary Clinton mask but that seemed cliché so I decided to go old school, like Billy the Kid (in a track suit, Jersey style) or at least something along those lines. I came around the corner from the jewelry store and I started getting nervous. I knew physically that I was safe but mentally I still needed to psych myself up. I didn't have a getaway plan but I wasn't worried about the police. It isn't as if they would start shooting at me in Georgetown, there were too many people around. Rich people.

I put the bandanna over my head and sprinted into the store. There were a few employees in the store and I ran right at a lady who appeared to be in her 60s wearing a pinkish business suit. I looked her in the eyes and with one downward punch I broke open the case with the Rolexes in them. Like a dumbass I didn't remember to bring a bag or anything else to carry them in, so I unceremoniously dropped them into my pocket. There was a case of necklaces next to them so I busted it open and grabbed them as well. I was only able to get four of them before I needed to leave. When I stuffed them into my warm-up pants pockets I felt them get tangled. Even though I knew I should've been more focused, I thought to myself about what a pain the ass it was going to be to untangle them later.

As I turned to leave I heard the magnetic clips on top of the door shut and then the alarm went off. They had locked me in. Whichever employee was responsible for hitting the security alarm had unknowingly locked everyone in with a monster who was perfectly willing and capable of killing everyone in the store. I just wanted to leave. I didn't know why the employee was trying to be a hero. The employees wouldn't be responsible for paying for the merchandise because the business insurance would cover it.

I punched the glass door right in the center. It cracked a little but so did my hand, which hurt a lot more than I thought it would. I could feel my bones mending as I tried to shake the pain away. I glared at the older lady. I didn't think she was responsible because since I was there she hadn't moved a muscle. Out of everyone in the store, she seemed the least heroic and the most likely to have a heart attack, but I had to be pissed at someone.

A few steps from the door, I picked up some speed and slammed into the entrance with my shoulder. It bulged out but didn't break all the way through. My bandanna started to slip so I pulled it up over my nose. A crowd was beginning to form outside.

I backed up again and gave myself a little more room. I took a few steps and busted through the window. My momentum carried me out over the sidewalk and I plowed shoulder first into a parked car, cracking the passenger side window and putting a huge dent in the door. The force of the crash caused my bandanna to fall down around my neck. I pulled it up and then picked myself up off the ground. The crowd looked at me like I was an alien coming out of a spaceship. A teenage girl was raising her phone to take a picture of me, so I plowed past her and took the phone in the process. I knew the jewelry store had cameras but there was no reason to add to the footage.

I started jogging down the street but my pants were bulging at the pockets and every step caused the jewelry to bash into my thighs. I heard sirens and I knew I needed to find a place to hide out for a bit and change. I found a boutique men's suit shop and strolled into it as casually as I could.

"May I help you sir?" said an older guy behind the counter wearing a blue three-piece suit and stylish black-framed glasses.

"Uh," I said. "I need a suit, quickly."

"Quickly?" He was looking at something on the counter, and when he responded he looked at me over the top of his glasses.

"Yeah, uh, my girlfriend's parents are in town and I have to go meet them. I totally forgot about it and now I'm running late."

"I see. Over here please." He waved me over to stand on top of a carpet-covered box that had three mirrors surrounding it.

"What are you looking for?" he asked as he measured me.

"The works."

A police car flew past the store with its siren wailing. The guy looked up from his measurements and looked me. Then he went back to measuring me.

He outfitted me with a three-piece suit that resembled his with a black tie and a black pair of shoes.

"Can I leave my running gear here and come back for it?" I said. "I'm very late and I don't have time to go home."

"I'm closing soon, but if you can pick them up tomorrow that would be fine."

"Okay, thank you. You're a lifesaver."

The outfit cost me a thousand dollars for the suit and another thousand for the silence fee. I wanted to question him about the silence fee but when I started to open my mouth he pointed at the security camera directly behind him. I had maxed out the remaining credit on my emergency card.

When I left the store, I felt like I had been robbed a bit but also like I was king of the world. The jewelry didn't make as much of a bulge in my pockets because I was able to split it up to more pockets. I put on a big, gold Rolex. It weighed quite a bit and I considered keeping it for myself, but getting the money for it was more important.

I went up to U Street to people watch. They would duck in and out of bars, and generally be ridiculously happy to see friends that they had seen a week before. I was jealous of them. Not angry jealous, sad jealous. I had lost most of my friends in DC. I didn't lose them all at once, they faded away, one by one. My friends back home didn't really know that that I had went through a change so there wasn't a growing chasm like there was in DC. I guess my friends in DC thought I was ignoring them or something else and had moved on. One of the hardest things to get used to while living in DC is that the city is very transient. People come for internships and get some experience to put on their resume and then go home or somewhere more affordable.

Walking down the street, a few blocks from my house, I noticed two men sitting in a black SUV. My first thought was that they were waiting for someone, but their lights were off and they weren't talking. A few weeks before I had seen the other guy wandering around a few blocks from my house and I started being extra cautious coming home. I tried to chalk it up to paranoia but the feeling that they were coming for me wouldn't go away. Some part of me knew that they were looking for me.

They had known where I lived for a while, and it was only a matter of time before they came after me. I was okay standing up for myself but I didn't want anything to happen to my friends. If they knew I was a vampire, all they would have to do is wait until the daylight hours and I wouldn't have a way to protect myself.

They were parked under an elm tree and the glow from the streetlight didn't penetrate their tinted windows.

In the month that had passed since Cecil came to my house, I had grown stronger. I didn't have a tingle in my fangs so I knew that they weren't vamps. I needed to make a strong statement and get these guys off my back.

After a running start, I jumped into the tree they were parked under. Unfortunately it didn't help my position much. The SUV didn't have a sunroof to jump through and even if I did and I went headfirst I would crash into the console between the seats.

I jumped out of the tree and landed on the driver's side. I punched through the window and landed a solid punch to the driver but the force was diminished because the glass was laminated.

The guy on the passenger side picked up a high-intensity halogen spotlight and shined it in my face. I was blinded and I could smell my skin starting to smoke. I started to open the door when the driver unexpectedly opened the door and hit me in the chest with it. He caused me stumble backward into the street. As I was getting my eyesight back, I heard the horn of a car and the squealing of the brakes.

A car coming down the street hit the open driver side door and then hit me. I was glued to the door by force and for a few moments I was holding onto the door while on top of some woman's hood. I remember noticing how wide her eyes were and for a moment I thought her eyes would pop out of her head. Then she slammed on her brakes and

I didn't care about her eyes any more. The door and I went our separate ways while airborne. I would love to say that I was able to land on my feet with some vampy awesomeness but instead I tumbled down the street like I was doing the world's fastest demonstration of the Stop, Drop, and Roll.

I picked myself up off the street. The SUV was going in reverse without the driver's side door. I waited a few moments as the painful process of my bones healing started. My skin started to tickle in a bad way as it scabbed over then healed. One of my legs was dangling limp but it mended itself along with my ribs and my shoulder. I couldn't believe that motherfucker caused me to get hit by a car.

They were perpendicular to the street because they were trying to turn around and go the other way. In the process, they bashed a car that was parked behind them while they were backing up.

They weren't going to get away that easy. My leg and shoulder had healed enough to be able to jump onto their car, so I did. I landed on their windshield and I saw the spotlight go on my legs. Fortunately my pants were still covering a majority of my legs so there was only sharp pain from the light coming into the small pinhole tears in my jeans.

I had enough of that fucking light. I reached around through the passenger side window and scratched at the guy's face until I got my hand on the spotlight. The car lurched forward and we were starting to pick up speed. The driver cut sharp on a corner in an effort to launch me off of his car. Once again I was airborne. I had the spotlight in my hand and I accidentally shined it in my face, temporarily blinding myself as I rolled down the street.

I got up and broke the spotlight on the pavement in the street. I was going to chase after them but I was exhausted.

They understood that I wasn't happy with them stalking me.

I thought to myself that the next time they come after me, they had better do a better job. I had no doubt in my mind that they would.

CHAPTER 17

I told Andrew and Anne that I was going to move home because my mom was sick. Anne generously offered to let me keep my place at a reduced rate but I declined.

I was starting to experience time on a different level than mortals. Everything for us moved faster including time and I didn't want to make any commitments. Instead of living day to day we lived month to month mainly because of our feeding habits. Also we didn't have to be anywhere. It was like the way that summer flew by when I was little ,but now every day had the same freedom. When you're immortal months and even years can pass without noticing.

Andrew didn't say much but I think he was relived because he wouldn't have to cover for me any more. He never did find out that in addition to having a murderer under his roof he also had a jewelry thief and a drug dealer's goon.

I got in touch with John through his people and we met on a bench in Lincoln Park. People jogged around us in the cool summer night while dogs jumped on each other and sniffed each other's butts. We were meeting a little closer to my house than I cared for but I figured that if his rival drug dealer knew where I lived then he would as well.

I handed him a Whole Foods bag with the stolen jewelry at the bottom of it. I figured that the cops wouldn't notice something so suburban.

"This is some interesting merchandise." He said, "It would have been more subtle to drive a semi into the building and then run off with it."

"Yeah, maybe next time," I said.

"They're scratched a bit and clearly they aren't still in the boxes so it makes it a little more difficult to sell."

"Shit. I should've asked if they could gift wrap them for me."

He smiled a little for, I think, the second time.

"I'll give you three grand for all of them."

"Come on. Help me out a little here. How about five?"

I wanted to make my money back and a little on top if possible.

"All right, five it is. I'll make it seven if you can help my guys run an errand."

"I really can't. I don't know how you do what you do but I need to chill out a bit. The police are looking for me because of Leanne Washington, killing some guy up north and now the jewelry store."

"Ah yes. You have been rather busy. I'm sure the jewelry store incident raised some eyebrows with some of the members of the Council but I will assure them that you are leaving and plan on taking it easy until then. I won't regret doing this for you, will I?"

"No. Not at all."

"Come over to the car with me." Then we headed over to his SUV. I was a little worried that I was going to get the trunk treatment like Charlie. The trunk popped and he reached in, pulled out a cooler and handed it to me.

"Keep this cold and it will be good for about three weeks. To be safe, you should probably ditch the leftovers after two weeks. There are very few things that are worse for us than bad blood."

I peeked into the cooler and saw bags of donor blood under an inch deep layer of ice.

"Thanks." I smiled at him, showing my fangs. Now I didn't have to worry about leaving a trail of dead people across the country.

Then he handed me a card and said, "If you find yourself in Harrisburg, Montana for any reason, visit this guy." The card said Torin Connaker and it had an address underneath. "He's an interesting character and he'll teach you a thing or two about being a vampire. He's over a thousand years old."

"Thanks, I appreciate it. I appreciate all the help you've given me."

He smiled and then got in the car. I watched his taillights drive into the night.

CHAPTER 18

I contacted Simon through John to let him know that I would be heading to Alaska. Simon told me that I was free to come and go as I please but that it was customary to speak to the Council before leaving their jurisdiction for good. They would also contact the new jurisdiction so they could prepare for another vampire living there. Also if I didn't arrive they would know.

Once again Simon arranged to pickup me at Lincoln Park with Roger driving. It was déjà vu all over again. Simon handed me the bag to put over my head and I did.

"It saddens me that you are leaving, Stephen," Simon said to me through the bag. "We were getting used to having a cub around."

"A cub?" I asked.

"It started out as a joke among vampires and for some reason it stuck. Mainly because lion prides have more females than males, like us. Lions leave prides to become nomads or to join other prides but females tend stay in the same area with each other. Young males always leave their original pride and rarely they return, but females always return, if only for a visit. I suppose to you modern folks it sounds sexist or some other bit of silliness but that's the way it is. There isn't malice in the terms."

"I plan on coming back," I said defiantly. When I said it I meant it at the time, but it didn't take long to realize that I didn't have much to come back to. The people that tied me to the area would die in a relatively short time it in the terms of an immortal. "I don't really want to leave our pride, but I have to go home because my mother is sick."

"One of the hardest times in your new life is watching your family and friends die one by one. At some point we've all had to cast off the vestiges of our old lives." He said. It sounded like he was facing me but with the hood on I wasn't completely sure. It would have been nice to see his eyes when he was telling me that. "If you are like most of the others before you, after your time of passage into the new world, you will want to wander a bit, wondering what to do with yourself. If you want to come back, please do."

"How will I get in touch with you?"

"Just show up. We will know." Then the car stopped and he got out. I sat there for a moment and waited for Roger to let me out. When Roger took the bag off of my head, Simon was gone. I wouldn't see him again for a long time.

The Council members were sitting in a big room that was more like a corporate conference room than anything else.

They weren't sitting three across like they had been on the judge's bench. The head female judge sat in the middle of the table, the lone male sat at the head of the table. The other female judge sat on the same side of the table as me but lounging in a chair against a far wall.

"I hear you are leaving us?" the head judge asked me in an informal, almost pleasant tone.

"Yeah. I have to go home and say goodbye to my mom." I was trying to make eye contact with all three of them at but they were sitting too far apart and it was like watching a tennis match so I settled on the head judge.

Then the male spoke. "It will be difficult but you mustn't change your mother."

"I know." I sighed without thinking about it.

"How do you plan on getting up there?" His voice was low and gravelly like he had spent an eternity smoking.

"I'm going to drive. It will give me and the dog a chance to see the country. Timing a flight based on the sun is tricky and if something happened during the flight I might get trapped on the plane."

"That is a good plan. The less people that you are around you the better." Then he looked at the head judge indicating that he didn't have anything more to say.

The head judge looked at me for a moment. "We will get in touch with the other Councils to let them know that you will be travelling through other districts and finally staying in Alaska for a bit. Lastly, you should know that we gave Charlie way more chances than other councils would have. In some districts the first vampire she created without permission would have been grounds for the death penalty. "

"Okay. Thank you." Then the door opened and Roger was standing there waiting with the bag in his hand. I looked at the three of them separately and tried to smile but nothing came out.

I left the room and Roger handed me the bag when we got to the car. I put it on and we drove off.

The next day the phone rang. The number came up as private so I figured it was either John or someone calling from Capitol Hill.

"Hello?" I said, a little distracted. The moment that I woke up the dog was ready to be fed. Diablo kept walking in front of me trying to herd me towards the kitchen to fill her bowl.

"Okay, okay," I said to Diablo. "Take it down a notch."

"Yes," I said, "Hi. Hello?"

"Hello Stephen, this is John. When you told me that you are leaving DC, I made peace with our friends that we had some problems with." He was pretty good at being coy on the phone because he suspected his phone was tapped.

"I'm glad to hear it," I said. "Do I play any part in the agreement?"

"Yes, albeit a small one. You can't ever come back to DC once you leave. If so then it will be open season on all of us. You don't plan on coming back, do you?"

"No. Not for a while."

"That is good. In exchange they will leave your friends alone."

"Sounds good to me."

"Besides, mortals don't have a long life span. Particularly the ones in my line of work." He made a heh, heh sound. "Until we meet again." Then he hung up.

On my last day, I had a small dinner with my old DC friends. Andrew told everyone that I had his wife to make a special dinner at home for me, which is why I wasn't eating. I didn't want to make a big deal about leaving because people left DC all the time. I had ten times more friends come and go in DC than friends who chose to stay. I had to divorce myself from my mortal life. I couldn't continue to kill people in a city with over 10,000 cameras. My friends were going to grow old and have families. I was stuck in time.

I had to say goodbye to my family in Alaska, not just my mom. I wanted to see them for one last time and then it would be over. It would've hurt my mother too much to disappear without seeing her again.

When I was little, my mom used to make me promise that I wouldn't ever die before her. It seems strange to say that now but for a few years I had a couple of friends die in accidents and it worried her immensely. Now that she is going first I knew that I was on the raw end of the deal.

Growing up I used to love watching cowboys on TV. My favorite part of the show was when the cowboy rode off into the sunset. Instead of riding off into the sunset like a hero, I drove west, away from the sunrise, like a villain.

ABOUT THE AUTHOR

Clayton Hanson was born and raised in Alaska. He enjoys naps and pizza. For the past three years he has worked as a writer and editor for a news service providing analysis and information about Congress in Washington, DC.
He is currently working on his second novel, Ms. Remorse. He can be found at Facebook.com/Hanson.Clayton and on Twitter @SnuffyMcDuffy.

www.ingramcontent.com/pod-product-compliance
Lightning Source LLC
Chambersburg PA
CBHW071257130626
46556CB00003B/1359